Papercut

M. NOVAK

1

The Jenson family was sitting in the tiny, magnolia-painted kitchen.

The room was small in the way that lives are small; hemmed in from all sides.

The tour of the village had been Peter's idea, born of desperation. He was miserable because his son, Simon, was miserable, wrenched as he had been, unceremoniously, from his lovely life in London and dumped (as Simon put it), into the middle of nowhere.

It was true that the village of Constance, did indeed seem to be unusually distant from any livelier town. Bucolic fields stretched in all directions, as far as the eye could see. Constance was, however, unfortunately close to the factory that the company that Peter worked for had just constructed and opened on land bought for a pittance from a local, slightly-senile farmer.

Peter had been sent to get it up and running and then to manage it. As an incentive the Jenson family had been offered 'free' accommodation in the twee cottage, that they were currently slumped in, for the length of their stay.

Simon was slouched on one rickety wooden chair, his sprawling legs stretched out across the burgundy ceramic floor tiles. There was no space for him here, was how he felt. At fifteen, his limbs were suddenly too long and the unusually tiny, high rectangular windows in that kitchen induced in him an undercurrent of anxiety.

His older sister, Poppy, a fresher at university many miles away in another part of England, did not, Simon thought bitterly, have to suffer the indignity of the sojourn in Constance. Once more, she had managed to get away with it.

In Simon's petty and jealous teenage brain, Poppy was always getting away with it. This was just one more, albeit massive, example.

"I've heard they do a quirky little tour of the village, to make new residents feel more at home." Peter was saying, forced bonhomie in his tone.

It was Saturday morning at the end of August. Half-opened boxes still cluttered the cottage but the kitchen was empty of their possessions still, bar some necessities, like a hotel room waiting to be occupied. A smell festered, of other people, damp and unloved.

Simon's mother and Peter's wife, Bernice, tried to paint a smile on her face. It emerged stilted, a half-grimace. Bernice had not wanted to move to Constance either, especially as it was for an indeterminate period. For some time now, even before Peter had mentioned his promotion and the obligatory move, Bernice had not been feeling right within her own skin.

However, she too, had enjoyed a full life in London and now she was surrounded by dullness, greenery, and cows. But it was not that, or at least not only that. At the core of Bernice, a sense of unease had gradually blossomed.

"Who told you about this 'quirky' tour?" Simon put heavy, sarcastic emphasis on the word 'quirky.'

Peter's determined smile faltered a bit, as if in memory of a lie.

"A man in the shop when I was buying the paper." That much was true, though actually the man had himself been strange. Peter didn't admit that. There was only the one shop in the village, right next to the pub. It was a dusty convenience store which sold a bit of everything and yet nothing that had been truly useful in the last decade, except for a painfully basic grocery selection.

"Saturday afternoon is the tour, usually, if we want it." Peter continued bravely whilst his wife and son stared at him. "I have to call the man who does it and he will put us on the list of participants."

"Who is this man?"

"The local pastor apparently," Peter shrugged. "Shall I make the call?"

2

The Jensons were the only people on the list and the only people on the tour.

They met outside the village church and Peter was only slightly surprised to note that the man who had told him about it in the first place, the strange-looking man in the shop, was the same person, the pastor, who was leading the tour.

Peter felt a glimmer of unease, but told himself to keep an open mind. He did not say anything to Simon or Bernice. They were miserable and sceptical enough as it was.

The church was obviously run down and huge but not ornate in the slightest. More than anything it resembled a school hall or some kind of town hall, grey, rain-flecked concrete and plywood, utilitarian and cold. From the outside it did not resemble a church at all, and for the first time, Simon's interest was piqued as he stared at it.

The sun was flirting weakly from behind fast-moving clouds but a cold wind slithered beneath their city clothes. They looked like tourists, standing there in the carpark where there were no cars, in front of huge wooden doors. They were tourists.

A massive white metal sign, on the doors of the church, shouted: 'SILENCE AT ALL TIMES'

The man, the pastor, who had bushy black eyebrows over deep-set grey eyes, introduced himself as Robert. He was not a large man, smaller and much scrawnier than both Peter and Simon and of an indeterminate middle age. He could have been anything from forty to seventy. There was, about him however, an intensity when he spoke that was somehow disconcerting. His manner reminded each individual family member of something or someone that they had witnessed before; in London or in a dream or in a nightmare. It was a flicker of a thought or a memory and then it vanished.

Robert was wearing the sort of jeans worn by a grandfather and a fishing jacket against the wind, of a shiny, frayed, deep river green. With a half-smile that fell just short of friendly in the normal way, Robert told the family that the previous church had been bombed badly and destroyed in the second world war. A freak bomb had landed on it. Freak because that village was not a natural target obviously. In fact, they had hosted many evacuees during that same war precisely because Constance, deep in the English countryside, was supposed to be a haven from the bombing in London at the time.

"It was my father who was in the church when it was bombed. He was the resident pastor at the time."

All three mentally recalculated Robert's age and Peter nodded sombrely.

"That must have been shocking for you and your family."

Robert shrugged, turning away.

"I was a very small boy then and things like that were happening in the country all the time. People just got on with it."

"Not like now." He added sharply. "Too much fuss now!"

He turned his cold grey eyes onto Simon as he said that, but then gave an offhand chuckle.

"Anyway, after the war the church was rebuilt with the uninspiring materials they had at hand. It was a bit of a downgrade from the original, but beggars can't be choosers and what not, as they say! My uncle ran it and then my cousin and for some years now, it has been my domain."

"It runs in the family, your…the…" Peter faltered.

"It's a calling, yes, and my family has been blessed." He gave a small pompous nod. "The Church of the Divine is our legacy."

"Anyway, shall we move on? There's plenty to see!"

3

There being 'plenty to see' turned out to be a bit of an exaggeration to put it mildly.

Robert took them to the miniature 'high street' in Constance and they stood in front of the nondescript pub (The Hare and the Raven) and the village shop where Robert had, just that morning, made Peter's acquaintance. The pub had several dead flowers in planters attached to its windows. Some faded half-baked graffiti adorned a damp patch of wall.

Robert waved his green clad arm down the tiny street and pointed out a chemist, a tool shop which specialised in fishing supplies (he was enthusiastic about that one), and a surgery housed in a normal Victorian terraced house.

"Of course, our local GP is ancient, he's very rarely there, any serious problems we have to go to Cavershall." He muttered this vaguely. Clearly, Robert was far more interested in the fishing supply shop than in the health of the village. Bernice meanwhile jolted awake and felt her internal spirits droop further.

"Really? There's nothing closer than Cavershall if there's a medical emergency?"

Cavershall was well over an hour away down winding country roads. The family knew this already as most of the workers in the factory would commute from there. Peter had told Bernice that several times. Bernice was already concerned about the remoteness of Constance. Her tone was alarmed then, and Robert narrowed his eyes at her.

"No need to be alarmed dear" his own voice was meaty and condescending. "People have lived in Constance for many years without incident. My own wife used to work as a nurse many years ago and is skilled at giving advice."

"A nurse?" Bernice tried to keep the scepticism out of her voice. She was not sure why it was there, only that she did not find this man credible.

"I see. You said she used to work as a nurse, what does she do now?"

Robert fixed his cold eyes upon her once more. There was something unforgiving about his gaze and Bernice felt a sudden desperate pang of homesickness for London and for the people she knew there.

"Sarah helps me within the church." He said smoothly with the grating smugness still in his voice.

"There is always so much to do, what with the cleaning and the administration and the organising."

He smirked suddenly and under the intensity of his grey gaze fixed onto her face, Bernice found herself twitch and fidget. An uncomfortable itchy heat rose within her body and she felt it settle like blusher on the skin of her cheeks.

"I find that women are best suited to be helpers, always."

Robert turned away then to wave his arm across the vista of some distant fields. He had moved onto Simon.

"You'll be attending the high school in Tensit, just like my son did no doubt."

"You have a son?" Simon blurted out. He could not imagine such a rigid-seeming man with a child, could not imagine any softness within.

"Oh yes, but he's in his late twenties now. Jacob has…" He paused, frowning slightly. "He has just returned from the Seminary. I am hoping he will carry on in my footsteps eventually, that is the plan."

For the first time, a glimmer of insecurity entered his pompous tone, and Bernice and Simon glanced at each other and raised their eyebrows in fleeting solidarity.

"Seminary? Is that where people study to be priests?"

"Priests or Ministers, yes. We are protestants, of course, I'm sure you realised that." The supercilious tone was back, confidently in place.

4

"I am looking forward to seeing you all at our Sunday service, of course."

Simon squirmed miserably. The family had, in London for years, attended their local, very laid-back, Church of England Church. It had been linked to Simon and Poppy's primary school and they had known everyone who attended. It had been the real focal point of their community throughout the years with the various feast days and celebrations providing often lonely, disparate Londoners with an opportunity to bond with other people, wherever they originated from. Simon could not imagine Roger's dour establishment providing the same sense of peace, especially not with him at the helm.

They were all standing behind the church then, facing the village cemetery. There were some gnarled old trees but overall, an uninspiring oblong of land. The damp tomb stones seemed to retain the memory of centuries of rain and grizzled people in black in sombre procession with their hands clasped behind their backs and their chins lowered. The ugly blockish church and its unattractive surroundings tried to drag Simon, so it seemed, into a past era full of glum, sour people that he had no interest in and certainly did not want to revisit.

He felt, like his mother, a pang of homesickness for the confident, edgy youth with the air of rebellion about them, always bounding through the fashionable streets of London.

Simon had never once been part of any cool set, but he would far rather be on the fringes of one, an uncool onlooker, than pulled in to contemplate whatever mind-numbing greyness this was.

"There's supposed to be a ghost in the church." Robert announced then, surprisingly. Was he making it up? Simon wasn't sure. Perhaps he could read the room, saw they were uninterested, unimpressed by the village, disappointed by the 'tour,' although, of course, they had not been expecting much. Maybe he was trying to keep their attention, for whatever reason.

Robert continued: "People have heard a strange clanging noise supposedly coming from the storage space, an oversized cupboard that we have attached to the kitchen at the back of the church. It's an old wives tale, I'm sure. I, personally, have never heard anything untoward, all the thousands of times that I have been there."

Robert seemed to imply that he was too smart to believe in such foolishness, but that his parishioners were more ignorant.

"Who's heard it then?" Simon was interested.

"Various people throughout the years. The ghost never seems to make itself known when the church is full, funnily enough." Robert snorted in a dismissive manner. "Some of the ladies who have helped prepare the flowers and clean the church before the services and after, through the years, they have apparently, according to them, heard the weird, unexplained noises. They were scared by them, of course, but I can't say that I…"

"Anyone else?" Interrupted Simon.

Robert eyes flickered with annoyance.

"Kids too, but kids, well, who believes children?"

Peter had long since lost interest in the conversation and had wandered off a short distance. From where he stood in deep, lonely contemplation, the main street of the village was just visible, the pub in profile.

Peter was feeling the burden of responsibility. The new factory was proving more of a headache than anyone had anticipated and there had been an abundance of technical and administrative issues, many still unresolved. Truth be told, he had not been listening to Robert at all, throughout the entire length of the short tour, his mind had been elsewhere. Peter worried constantly that he had taken on more than he could chew, and, well, uprooting his family like this, it wasn't going well so far, not well at all if the miserable expressions on their faces were anything to go by.

At the time that his boss had sold him the move, Peter had been elated at the prospect of the promotion that came with it and specifically the wage increase, and had not given the move as much careful thought as it merited.

Of course, on the part of his boss, that too had been a tactical move. There was no way that anyone could have been persuaded to move to Constance without a substantial pay rise and promotion, so naturally he had dangled that in front of Peter like a lovely juicy carrot. His boss had suspected also that Peter was struggling financially, which was true.

The tour, such as it was, seemed to have come to a natural end and the three members of the Jenson family bid a polite goodbye to Robert and trailed back to their unlovely cottage through the strange, (to them), silence of the countryside. Even in the relative warmth of an English summer, the cottage emitted a pungent damp smell, more noticeable after the fragrant outside air, and the thick walls were clammy to the touch.

5

Bernice, in particular, found the cottage more than vaguely repulsive. She had loved the clean modern lines of their town house in London, this all felt…uncomfortable. It felt like a holiday let, but in this case, there was no foreseeable prospect of packing up and going home and letting out a sigh of relief at being cosy again.

Several non-eventful, lethargic, days had passed in the cottage. Simon, having been temporarily distracted by the story of the ghost in the dank, ugly church was now back to brooding about his sojourn in this tragic village and specifically about his pending enrolment in his new high school.

Tensit was a very slightly larger village situated approximately five miles away. It housed a smallish high school which catered for all the teens from the surrounding tiny villages and hamlets. One of Simon's most valid arguments against moving there had been that the quality of teaching would be way lower than what they were used to in London.

"What sort of half-arsed teacher would want to move to the middle of nowhere?" He had howled despairingly when the prospect of the move had first been put before him.

Bernice had tried to reassure him through gritted teeth.

"All the teachers are of the same standard, I'm sure. Some people move to the countryside because they genuinely love it!" She told him brightly, although Bernice herself was not convinced.

There was less than a week until the new school year kicked off. That meant that there was a looming and immediate prospect of a uniform shopping trip in Cavershall, the following day or the next. Nobody could quite face it. The prospect of uniform buying seemed to somehow underline the depressing finality of the move.

Simon was halfway through his GCSE course, which was another of his well-versed arguments as to why the change of schools was a terrible idea. He brought it up then again, the same lament in the same despairing tone. Bernice sighed heavily once again.

"Look! It's not ideal for any of us. Not even your father actually wanted to move to some remote village, we all know it's going to be difficult, and yes, probably for you, most of all because of your age and school and all the rest of it, but, it will get better, I promise. In school, they'll see you as the cool kid from London!"

Simon snorted.

"They will not. I have never, ever, been the cool kid, not once!"

"Well." Bernice chuckled although it sounded fake even to her own ears. "You have never been to a country school before. They'll all be country bumpkins and impressed by you, I'm sure."

"You have never been to a country school either mum." Simon commented sourly. "I'm not sure the country bumpkin cliché is true anymore. They'll be rough, if anything, and pick on me because I'm different. Different in ways that I won't even realise until I am there."

Bernice stayed silent then. She didn't have the heart to argue with the boy. He was probably right, at least partially. She felt a sad exhaustion descend on her and lowered her gaze dolefully to contemplate the inside of her coffee cup. They were both sitting at the kitchen table. The walls were tight around them. Silence came to them then, a heavy fog of it. They were annoyed with each other and themselves, both. The atmosphere was gritty and uncomfortable and Simon squirmed restlessly within it.

Bernice was thinking of a specific park in London where she always used to walk whenever she had any free time. It was one of those quirky, surprising parks with curvy ramshackle paths and amazing blooms and hidden undisturbed nooks. You would think, Bernice thought then, that the actual countryside would trump any urban park, and yet somehow it did not.

6

It had been less than a year ago, in the early Autumn of the previous year that Bernice had literally bumped into Alex in that very park.

Upon opening the front door that day she had realised that it was unexpectedly cold with a sudden biting bitter chill, against which Bernice had piled on a random and unmatching selection of outerwear, before taking herself out for a walk to clear her head.

Alex had one of those fluffy off-white dogs which were fashionable at that time in that middle-class part of London. Bernice would later learn that it was called a labradoodle, but she did not yet know that when the dog, still a puppy, hurled itself against her whilst in pursuit of a squirrel. It did not hurt Bernice but she was stressed and had been deep in her own thoughts and had emitted a kind of strangled gasp of shock.

Alex, to his credit, was effusively apologetic as he came rushing up and grabbed his dog by the collar, admonishing him. Alex looked, at that moment, as messy as Bernice felt. Bernice felt bedraggled inside and out.

Peter's job, in the lives of their family, had always taken precedence. Bernice's job, as a tutor, was perceived, she believed, as little more than a hobby, whilst she also maintained their home singlehandedly.

However, recently, aware that they were struggling financially as a family, Bernice had been getting more and more work from the local adult education college. They had employed Bernice to teach basic literacy to adults who couldn't or who could barely read. It was not a particularly easy or relaxing gig.

The cohort she was teaching included a not insubstantial group of ex-prison inmates who were taking the literacy course to, supposedly, make them more employable. They were being forced to attend Bernice's course against their will and many were very unhappy about it and did not bother hiding that fact.

Just that same morning, Bernice had experienced an unpleasant episode with a youth called Ryan. Ryan was nineteen but looked younger. His impish, cheeky appearance, however, belied a more deeply rooted malaise. Bernice did not know what Ryan had been 'in for' but if she was being totally honest with herself, she knew that she feared him on some basic, visceral level.

Bernice had been brooding on Ryan and on what had occurred that morning when she had collided with Alex's dog, and she reacted with greater fury than she would normally have done. Even as Alex apologised incessantly, she persisted in scowling and mumbling darkly about out-of-control dogs being on a lead. She knew that she was being unreasonable and that she should just let it go and yet somehow, her pent-up tension was being eased and released with this bout of stroppiness.

Alex found something attractive in the small, irate lady. Himself a successful architect, he was used to people being excessively and often slaveringly nice to him, all the time. It was refreshing to come across someone who clearly didn't care how important he was and wasn't interested in sucking up to him. He asked Bernice if she wanted to go for a coffee with him by way of apology.

Bernice stared at him for a minute in shocked silence. His grey scarf was wound about the lower part of his face so that only his large brown eyes were visible. They seemed sincere. The invitation, the situation itself, seemed so bizarre and unexpected and yet somehow could not have come at a better time or at a more opportune time for Bernice with the way she was feeling; neglected and frustrated and put upon.

The two of them walked to a small, ramshackle café situated in the centre of the park. It was the relaxed, cosy domain of mothers and toddlers who sauntered in to warm up after hours in the playground, of elderly people sitting huddled and lonely over solitary cups of tea.

The hot blast of air inside was a welcome relief and as Bernice began to remove her abundant layers, Alex realised that she looked older than she first appeared, and yet it did not matter to him.

She had what he needed.

7

Poppy had arrived in Nottingham weeks before the beginning of the university term. This was partly because her family were all relocating to Constance and she did not want to hang out in London alone, dragging out her stay with various friends. It made far more sense to Poppy to move on with the next stage in her life at the same time.

Also, and more significantly, because she hadn't done as well as expected in her A-levels, she had had to go through clearing. She had not predicted that she would land in Nottingham, and yet they had accepted her and now she had to somehow find herself some accommodation.

Originally, Poppy had planned to study English in Durham but now that she was in Nottingham, wandering about in the late summer sunshine, she told herself that she preferred it. The campus was amazing; a huge verdant park.

Whilst searching for a place to live, and repeatedly hounding the University accommodation office, Poppy was staying at a youth hostel in the very centre of the city, and this too gave her sojourn a festive, holiday feel.

Poppy knew only one person from her former school, not a friend, just a random girl, who would also be studying in Nottingham, but that girl, Tina, wasn't there yet and, in the meantime, Poppy hung around in the evenings with the foreign students who gathered in the brightly-lit canteen part of the youth hostel with cheap beer and snacks purloined from the cut-price supermarket nearby.

The foreign students, mainly German and Scandinavian were friendly enough but clearly baffled by Poppy's presence at their table and in their hostel.

"But if your family is in the UK, why don't you stay with them until your university starts?" Was an extremely common question from them. They were large and practical in the main, they wore clothes and shoes suitable for camping and hiking. The girls had scrubbed faces and barely anyone wore make up.

It was the early '90s though and Poppy had come up from fashionable London. She sat before them wearing heavy black eyeliner, black leggings, and massive shiny boots. Her hair was dyed peroxide blonde. She had dyed it relatively recently on a dare. It was growing out now, but the sight of the dry whitish split ends in the periphery of her vision brought about a pang of nostalgia for the friend who had dared her to dye it, in particular, and for London in general.

There were a few boys, mousy and sensible too in the main, but there was a black-clad gothic Polish boy who was greeted with the same subdued bafflement as Poppy was and the two perceived outcasts inevitably seemed to gravitate towards each other, at first anyway.

Unlike most of the others who were interrailing through Europe and just touring around the UK, Victor was there in Nottingham for three weeks to learn English.

He wasn't particularly happy about it. His face wore a permanent dark scowl which matched the vibe emitted by his clothing.

"I need the English for University." He told Poppy petulantly.

It was early evening and the two of them were sitting on the fringes of the larger crowd nursing cheap lukewarm cider. They had found that the cheap cider was more palatable than the cheap beer.

"I go in October."

"OK" Poppy nodded doubtfully. His English was poor. He spoke very little and seemed to understand even less. Although it was hard to tell as he didn't seem to like the other Europeans much and barely bothered communicating with them at all. It was only Poppy he tolerated and she thought that it was more because he thought they were similar outcasts rather than because of any more romantic motive.

8

"We need to get the uniform shop over and done with." Sighed Bernice. "I think we'll feel better once it's out of the way."

Simon nodded glumly. It wasn't as if he had anything better to do. It would be a relief to get out of that damp cottage temporarily if nothing else.

They had just the one middle-aged family car, and in anticipation of the uniform-buying trip to Cavershall, Peter had not taken it to work that day. Instead, somewhat stoically (and slightly to make a point about resourcefulness and resilience,) he had got up extremely early to catch the village bus which trundled slowly along village lanes before depositing him half a mile away from the factory. He turned a corner on foot in the hazy light and suddenly there it was, spectacular in its own way.

The huge utilitarian rectangle loomed from the landscape, rising up from the green blur of the countryside like a foreign alien, a spaceship-type thing, the burnished steel trim of the walls glinting in the weak sunlight emanating through the clouds.

There was something magnificent about it, Peter thought, a glimmer of pride rising within him, contemplating it as he stood there on the country road. Nobody would have predicted that Peter, as a small boy, would grow up to be partially responsible for such a huge operation, Peter himself least of all.

The drive from Constance to Cavershall was stressful for Bernice. Almost the entire route took them down narrow, winding, country lanes and Bernice could not bear to think what she resembled, some oversized rodent perhaps, hunched over, her hands gripping the steering wheel like claws, squinting through the windshield, and driving slower than she ever had in her life.

Simon made no secret of his frustration.

"If you carry on at this pace, we won't get there until this afternoon." He grunted miserably. He had his feet in their trainers up on the dashboard but Bernice didn't say anything. She had to pick her fights with him now. They had to be allies of sorts, both of them stranded in the countryside against their will. That was how she felt.

"This is nothing like driving in London, I'm not used to it. Most of these so-called roads are too narrow for two cars to pass each other even!"

Simon didn't say anything. He was staring out of the window at the thick green canopy without seeing it. In his imagination he was back in London, hanging out with his old friends there, he hadn't appreciated how happy he was at the time. He regretted that now.

Neither of them had expected much of Cavershall and they were not disappointed. Unlike Constance which with so tiny that no real judgements could be made about its character, beyond the fact that it seemed old-fashioned and quite unfriendly; Cavershall was rough around the edges and made no attempts to disguise the fact.

The high street seemed extensive for such a small town and quite a few of the usual big names, albeit the cheaper brands, were represented. In between them and the cut-price supermarkets however, there were abundant empty boarded up shop fronts, which always looked awful, like missing teeth. Graffiti adorned those filthy boards, not the arty kind. Simon's interest piqued briefly. They have gangs even here, he thought. There was a kind of concrete square positioned in front of the only department store There were some sad optimistic planters full of cigarette butts, some wooden benches, mainly broken. There was a small group of youths slouching on one of them, smoking. As Simon and Bernice approached, one of them glanced at them, his eyes cloudy and without focus.

"This is where we get your uniform, third floor." Stated Bernice at that moment, her voice as clear as a middle-class bell.

All of the youths looked up then, their straggly heads darting up like meerkats and Simon winced. Of course, he thought miserably, they would be going to his high school, it was inevitable. His card was already marked.

On the fringes of Cavershall, huge soulless council blocks marred the landscape. Simon noticed them when they drove in and when they drove out again. The bag with his uniform sat on the back seat of the car, a plasticky new smell emanating from it. Simon had felt embarrassed trying it on, overgrown and ridiculous. He had seen himself reflected in the eyes of the shop assistant, a woman with papery skin with the stench of cigarettes permeating from her.

9

The affair between Bernice and Alex had started slowly, via the medium of coffee.

On that very first day, inside the stuffy confines of the café in the park, Alex's dog had laid his chin on Bernice's knee within minutes of the waitress taking their order and Bernice had felt something within her start to melt. It had been so long since any physical affection had been shown her. At that point, it would probably have been more prudent to get her own dog than to embark on an affair. Maybe she was confused, maybe her emotions didn't properly distinguish between Alex and his dog, but Alex was being excessively sweet too, apologising profusely and trying to win her round. He was really going over the top.

The café itself was an unlikely location for a seduction it could well be said, and yet there was about it a messy, chaotic warmth. It oozed comfort. The two ladies who worked there were jolly and welcoming. There were babies and rosy-cheeked toddlers and friendly dogs. The whole scene was in stark contrast to the misery of Bernice's job and the sterility of Bernice's marriage. Furthermore, the pent-up aggression of Ryan and some of the others had transmitted to Bernice a kind of breathless permanent anxiety. Finally, right then, sitting opposite Alex, she felt once again able to breathe deeply in a normal manner.

Alex kept apologising until Bernice told him to stop and then they chatted normally, just like friends catching up after a long hiatus. Bernice found herself opening up about her job, if not yet about the loneliness of her marriage.

Unlike Peter, and quite bizarrely considering that he barely knew her, Alex exhibited concern that Bernice should be working in such dangerous conditions, under the constant threat of violence.

"Is there no one monitoring your students, supervising them as it were, no risk assessment?"

Bernice laughed.

"No, nothing like that. I guess they are considered to be safe with members of the public. They have been released from prison, after all."

"I don't think that means much, all sorts of dangerous people are released too early, that's well-documented. So, you don't feel safe, with Ryan in particular?"

"I don't ever feel completely safe, no, but it's just a feeling, no one is going to act on that!"

Alex nodded sombrely, his face creased with concern.

He had a lived-in sort of face, that was how Bernice described him to herself afterwards. He had more than the allocated amount of wrinkles and yet somehow, they suited him. Especially the crinkles around his eyes. He looked as if he smiled a lot. He looked like a warm friendly man.

They didn't officially arrange to meet again, but an hour later, as they were saying goodbye outside, the memory of warmth already fading from their bodies, Alex said:

"I tend to come here at this time every day."

Automatically, they both looked at their watches and caught each other's' eye and laughed. Once more they were swaddled against the cold and only their smiling eyes could be seen. The dog nuzzled against Bernice's leg and whined when she turned to leave. As she walked down the path away from there, she felt within her a chasm opening, already she missed them.

It was ridiculous, she knew.

That was how it began.

10

Poppy had gone to visit the University accommodation office for the umpteenth time. To her great surprise and relief, the frazzled girl who worked there told her that they might have something.
"Why might?"
"Well, we have had some issues with this particular landlord in the past, and you might not like it. It's not our best offering, I'm not going to lie."
Poppy sighed.
"Can I see it anyway and decide?"
The girl shrugged, stood up and manoeuvred herself into the denim jacket which was draped over the back of her chair.
"Sure, why not."
The accommodation office was on the edge of the university campus, but the girl led Poppy away from it, down bleak winding streets lined with industrial-type spaces, factories, and the like. Poppy was reminded suddenly of her father and his new factory and she wondered how the sojourn in Constance was going.
None of them had a mobile phone except for Peter and that was a work phone. Any phone call between Poppy and her family would have to go via the landline at the youth hostel. Truth be told, Poppy had felt detached from her family for some time. She wasn't desperate to talk to them, right then. She was quite happy to be navigating her life on her own at that moment. There had been a sour atmosphere between her parents for some time it seemed, and that had had an inevitable effect on the kids too. Probably it was her brother who Poppy missed the most although she was well aware that he resented her at that moment for having 'escaped,' illogical as it was.
The girl from the accommodation office kept walking and Poppy kept following. She was not a chatty girl clearly and did not give the impression that she wanted to talk. That was fine by Poppy who was deep in her own thoughts. She was deciding that she would take this room regardless of the condition. Victor was starting to freak her out a little bit. Whenever she walked into the youth hostel or came downstairs in the morning (it was fortunate that she shared a room with a Swedish girl), he was there, waiting for her. She couldn't pretend to ignore him either

as then he would just hover around anyway. It was increasingly disconcerting.

The girl kept leading the way. They had left the industrial streets and were now in an area teeming with tiny, grubby terraced houses all lined up in monotonous rows. Only a few of the owners had made an effort with brightly-coloured paint. Most were a uniform grey.

"This is not the best area." Said the girl cheerfully and Poppy sighed in agreement. Her spirits were dipping further with every step she took.

The pair arrived at a small row of shops. There was a newsagent, a pub draped in the usual ratty flags with a wooden sign creaking on the pavement outside. The Coach and Horses. The sign depicted an old-fashioned illustration of a gleaming fancy coach which had almost certainly never been seen around those parts. There was also a locksmith and a chemist with bars across the windows.

"Here we are." Said the girl.

"Where?" Asked Poppy bemused.

"It's on top of this locksmith shop. The guy owns the upstairs property." The girl gave Poppy a funny, concerned type of half-smile. Poppy would have cause to remember that smile later. She led the way into the shop and Poppy followed. Staying in the youth hostel, albeit with Victor, was now looking increasingly appealing.

The shop was dusty and crammed full of goods. It was the sort of shop that Poppy had always ignored completely throughout her life on the grounds that it contained nothing of interest to her. She looked at the oldish man behind the counter and was relieved to note that he looked, at first glance, harmless enough. He had a pale, pasty countenance, and watery blue eyes. He looked like someone's father. Not hers though. Poppy's father looked nothing like that. For one second, she missed him with a fierce pang.

The locksmith and the girl from the accommodation office exchanged brief stilted pleasantries, and then the man rifled through a drawer in front of him to locate an old-fashioned key which he held before him before heading to the back of the shop wordlessly.

No doubt expecting them to follow, which they did.

11

"Do you think it would show goodwill if we attended church this morning?"

It was early on Sunday but they were all already in the kitchen, sprawled there uncomfortably in their pyjamas. At some point in the night a pipe somewhere in the cottage had started clanging loudly and ceaselessly and no one had slept well.

"Never mind church," commented Bernice irritably, "Have you managed to get hold of a plumber?"

"Yes, he can't come until tomorrow."

" Well, surely there's got to be more than one!"

"Not that I know of. As it is, this one is coming from Tensit."

"For fucks sake!"

Peter glowered at his wife. He didn't like swearing.

"We may as well go to church." He sighed.

"I'm definitely not in the mood."

"Think of it as taking a positive step forward, socially, I mean."

"Maybe the clanging was the ghost!" Muttered Simon.

"What?" Peter scowled, stretching out his leg awkwardly. A sudden cramp had seized it.

"The story? The ghost in the kitchen of the church?"

"What story?"

"Never mind." Simon sighed too, (the family all seemed to spend a great deal of time sighing.) "We may as well go to church, it's not as if we have anything else to do."

He was thinking about the ghost more than anything else. He wanted to see the inside of that church. That story was a funny thing to make up. If someone were to make up a ghost, you'd think it would reside in a creepier location, the cemetery for instance, not a cupboard behind a kitchen.

Bernice nodded, resigned. Why not? She thought.

The family dressed as they would have done for the previous church they attended, that is casually, with a hint of smartness. However, it was immediately apparent from observing the meagre crowd gathered still in the parking lot that they were woefully underdressed; this lot really had come out in their Sunday best. They all looked as if they were dressed for an old-fashioned wedding or a christening.

Robert, looking completely different and much more polished than when they had previously seen him, came over to greet them.

"Sorry, I should have told you we believe in dressing up for church here." He smiled but his eyebrows were raised as if in incredulity and there was the same cold stiffness about him which they recalled from before.

Simon looked around as the crowd began to file into the church. Even the teenagers were stuffed into cheap polyester suits and traditional dresses as if they were actors in a play set in a much more conservative decade. There were relatively few of them and they hung their heads moodily. He wondered how many of them would be attending high school with him. They didn't look any more probable, in terms of candidates for friendship, than the vaguely sinister gang outside the department store in Cavershall. Albeit for entirely different reasons. This lot did not look dodgy in the slightest, just miserable and kind of spaced out.

Inside, the hall looked exactly like any school hall in the country. Even the smell was the same. It was a medley of damp and sweat and old food, except in this case the whole thing was overlaid by the flowery waxy aroma of multiple candles burning on the small stage, as well as by an overly sweet scent of decaying vegetation The candles were lined up, both on top of and beside a huge table which clearly served as an altar. Dotted about the hall, were various flowers and wilting greenery arranged poorly in vases.

Grey plastic chairs were arranged in rows to seat the congregation. Simon, Bernice, and Peter took the end of one of the back rows without consulting each other. Simon's eyes sought out the church kitchen, supposed residence of the ghost. Behind the altar and to the left was a door, he presumed that was where the kitchen was. It all seemed very improbable now that he was inside the dull, uninspiring space, that anything exciting would happen there, or indeed had ever happened there.

12

Poppy and the girl from the accommodation office followed the man as he went out of the back of the shop into a small back alley and from there opened a plain unassuming door, inside which was a staircase which led sharply upwards.

"You access this entrance from outside, you don't go through the shop." He instructed curtly.

"Right." Said Poppy nervously.

"There's a passage next to the shop." He turned to look at Poppy sharply with his blue eyes.

"OK."

Up the stairs they went, the carpet grimy and crunchy underfoot, and through another flimsy glass door which was unlocked and then there was a tiny hall, and leading off it a kitchen, a bathroom and two other doors, both shut.

"These are two of the bedsits, both occupied."

"By our students!" the accommodation girl turned to offer Poppy a reassuring half-smile which didn't quite reach her eyes.

"Your room would be upstairs." The landlord set off immediately up the next flight of stairs. Poppy glimpsed an old-fashioned boiler in a kind of enclave built off the stairs, and noticed the accommodation girl glance at it and raise her eyebrows with an expression of incredulity.

Another small landing with another bathroom, not too grim for a student house and two further closed doors, one of which the landlord unlocked with another, smaller key.

"This would be your room." He announced swinging open the door with a flourish.

The room was exceptionally small. It was a bit longer than the length of an average single bed and about twice the width. There was a single bed in it, in fact, made of the cheapest pine frame. Atop of which was a thin but relatively clean mattress. Next to the bed, in lieu of a bedside table, was the sort of desk which would have been suitable for the scribblings of a young child. Because of the lack of space, one would have to sit on the bed to write at the desk. Opposite the door and behind the pine headboard was a grubby window behind which the tatty flags of the Coach and Horses were clearly visible.

"They have a karaoke on a Saturday, apart from that they're quiet enough." Commented the landlord, as if that was the only issue that might have been worrying Poppy.

"Is there a chest of drawers or somewhere where I might store my clothes?" Asked Poppy timidly, although it was clear that not only was there not such an item, there also wouldn't be room for it.

The landlord made a gave a snort in reply, as if the question was absurd.

"I believe the previous tenant kept his clothes in boxes." He commented.

On the way back downstairs, they passed a girl with long straggly hair in hippyish garb. She smiled shyly at Poppy as she passed, large brown eyes crinkling merrily in the corners. The place couldn't be that bad if that girl lived there, reasoned Poppy somewhat illogically.

When they were alone again (Poppy had told the landlord that she would let him know), and heading back towards campus, the girl from the accommodation office told Poppy that they could find her something else.

"It wasn't that bad." Said Poppy.

The accommodation girl turned to give her a sombre but incredulous stare.

"Really?"

"Well…" Poppy was thinking of Victor. The thought of him, of the way he waited for her and watched her, oppressed her.

"I'll let you know soon." She said.

13

Robert's tone of voice droned harshly through the long sermon. In front of the Jensons, the congregation kept their heads bowed as they sat and stood repeatedly and sang tuneless hymns in wavering voices. Only Robert's voice rose lustily, as well as those of a scattering of other baritones who were seated in the front row alongside a plump lady and an awkwardly shaped youth.

Simon, bored out of his mind within minutes, and having lost interest in observing the door of the kitchen, had ample time to observe them and the rest of the congregation. It was quite hard to see the large lady and the youth clearly, however, as they were so far, in the front row and obscured by other bodies constantly rising to their feet. Simon looked, instead, almost instinctively, for people his own age. As he had told his mother, it was true that he had never been one of the 'cool' kids, but he was sociable enough in his way and liked to have a group of peers to chat to and hang out with.

The offerings in that church hall looked slim.

Two rows in front of the Jensons, there was a smartly dressed family consisting of mother, father and two teenage girls. All four looked as if they had dressed to take part in a play about churchgoing in the post war era. They all sported stiff, uncomfortable clothing in drab brownish colours, the sort of brittle, inflexible material that digs into your flesh. Simon could almost sense the rough, raspy fibres rubbing against his own tender skin. There was no need for it, he thought then, no need to be so uncomfortable. It was so unnecessary.

Both girls, Simon estimated one to be a bit younger than him and the other to be a bit older, wore their mousy brown hair in tight buns as if they were ballet dancers. The backs of their long white necks looked quite enticing to him, if he was honest. Both they and the woman whom Simon presumed was their mother, were extremely slim, bony even. Their father, however, was portly. From behind, the cut of his old-fashioned, tailored jacket dug unbecomingly into the rolls of fat on his back. Their mother had thin mousy hair, of the same shade as that of her daughters. It was arranged in a tight long plait which resembled nothing less than a tail of some straggly dry-skinned beast.

Simon spent a considerable chunk of the endless sermon trying to see the girls' faces, or at least their profiles, when they stood and sat on demand, folding their bodies neatly into the correct positions, like little robots.

There were other teenagers too who Simon could see, but they were boys, those that were nearby and visible, and less interesting to him. They too, were stuffed into and stifled by old-fashioned garments and were clearly unhappy about it. Although they rose and sat on demand and mouthed the words to the tuneless hymns, their expressions were mutinous, gloomy, or sad or a dazed mixture of all three.

The sermon was so long that Simon felt it would never end. He knew his parents felt the same, judging by the amount of fidgeting and sighing that was going on either side of him. By the time it did actually end, he had dozed off into a light snooze, his chin drooping to his chest. It was the footsteps of the people leaving that roused him, suddenly, and it was then he saw the faces of the two girls as they regarded him curiously as they walked by.

14

Bernice had waited three days before going back to the café in the park at the time that Alex had strongly hinted that he would be there.

Perhaps she would have even gone before had she not had to work. The surety that she would go was never in question. Since she had met Alex, she had felt a quickening within her, an excitement, such as she could not remember feeling since her youth, since she had first met Peter, in those heady, early days.

Of course, there was guilt, how could there not be? Although, oddly, it was only when she looked at her children that she felt it, not when she looked at Peter. Peter had long been a stranger to her; that was how she felt.

It was a bright sunny day but there was a chill to the air and a brisk wind. The café was completely full, both indoors and outside with people huddled at the outdoor tables, hunched uncomfortably over hot drinks, their fingers wrapped around them, seeking warmth. Dogs panted and wagged their tails and sniffed each other. The atmosphere was as busy and jolly as before and it was then that Bernice spotted Alex at a small table inside, by the window. He was looking straight at her.

She felt a jolt within, a shock to the heart and the nerves and without thinking, on autopilot almost, she hurried inside to be with him.

"I have been waiting for you." He said then, as she unwound the scarf from her neck and sat opposite him, her breath coming in short shallow gasps. His tone was different than it had been before, it was harsher. Politeness and formality had seemingly been dispensed with, at least partially, in that instant.

There was no time, Bernice felt, to worry about how she felt about that. A tiny sensible part of her brain was squirming and telling her to walk away, that this was her window to depart, her only window, but she stayed and sat down and ordered a cup of tea from a harried waitress.

Alex seemed to calm down then, now that she was there sitting opposite him, close to him, and he became more solicitous and friendly again, the way he had been on that first day. Bernice got lulled into it once more, so easily. There was his calculated charm and the way his eyes crinkled so becomingly at the corners; it was like slipping into a warm bath.

He talked much more than she did, about his designs and his projects and his plans. Seemingly, he had forgotten about Bernice's difficult job and about Ryan and how unpleasant he was. Or maybe he hadn't forgotten, but he did not ask Bernice about the situation and if it had improved. Bernice thought it was fair enough, it was time for him to talk, she herself had been given ample time to talk the first time they had met.

Alex's dog immediately stood from where it was lying under the table and rested his wet nose in Bernice's lap. She placed her hand on his soft tangled fur and only after, far too long after, did she wonder (it was too late by then), whether it was the dog she wanted, that dog or her own dog, rather than the man? Whether she ever wanted the man at all?

Still, Alex was being solicitous again and became kinder the more and the longer they spoke. Sometime much later he did ask her about Ryan and her job and how she felt about it all. They were in his flat by then, had just walked into it and he turned to her and asked her how things were.

As an afterthought.

His flat was a modernist cube it seemed. It was almost empty of furniture. There were metallic, solid surfaces and concrete floors painted white.

After, much later, when the pale sun had set, Bernice lay naked and cold and thought of her kids back in her, in their, warm, cosy kitchen roaming around, looking for food in the kitchen. When they were hungry, teenagers became like scavengers. Bernice thought of their faces, a bit spotty, a bit defiant and felt a pang. In front of her was the fleshy wall of Alexs' back.

He had fallen asleep immediately after, and Bernice had listened to the raindrops clatter against the glass of the windows.

15

On the Monday, Peter called a meeting at the factory for all the managers, the foremen, the entire management team. Everyone was new, the whole factory was brand spanking new, the machines bright and shiny and glinting in the weak sunlight pouring in at the enormous high windows.

The meeting was held on the Mezzanine, in a large room with huge windows, dazzling still, overlooking the factory floor. The floor was silent, the workers, the machine operatives were due to start the following day.

Peter was sitting at the head of the oval table which smelt of new plasticky things, even though it was supposed to be wood. He tried to hide his nerves, surprising nerves because he was not a man given to anxiety. However, at that moment for some reason, he found that his hands were trembling, very slightly but uncontrollably.

To the left of him sat a man, previously unknown to him, that had been allocated to him as his 'righthand man' according to his boss. It was unclear to Peter what the man's role officially was within the hierarchy of the factory. It had been Peter's initial understanding that Dennis would be his personal assistant, a glorified secretary, and yet Dennis's confidence and permanent supercilious expression seemed to suggest that he was much more important than that. More of a deputy manager to Peter's manager even.

In any case, Dennis did nothing for Peter's new inexplicable insecurity; whatever he said was greeted with a smirk or a grimace. Peter was spending most of his first days at the factory wondering how to get rid of Dennis. He seemed such an unlikely recruit for a factory. As well as being smug, he was jittery and easily bored. He belonged in some sales office in a big city, thought Peter. Maybe his presence there was due to a favour Peter's boss was granting to a golf buddy. That was the only reasonable explanation.

The rest of the management team seemed alright; dull and plodding but with the appropriate mind-numbingly boring interest in details and safety.

In fact, one of the portly, more senior managers was in the middle of an excruciatingly boring speech to do with health and safety and the parking facilities, when Samantha, Peter's new secretary came in, her high heels clicking, tap, tap on the floor. Everyone suddenly woke up and looked at her, their faces relaxing into expressions ranging from relief at the interruption to full-blown lust.

Unlike most of the employees of the factory who resided in Cavershall, Samantha lived in Tensit. Peter was not sure how he knew that fact, or indeed why it had stuck in his mind, but he thought of it then as he, and the rest of the men, watched Samantha struggle with an enormous tray full of glass jugs of coffee and milk and plates of fancy biscuits. The cups and saucers were already laid on a sideboard at one end of the room.

They all watched Samantha's bottom in a black pencil skirt, as she distributed the coffee and made murmured enquiries about milk and sugar. The health and safety speech was completely unheeded, and yet the man still droned on. Peter noticed that there was a fine sheen of sweat that lay atop Samantha's beige foundation and that her pink lip gloss was shiny. There was a smudge of black mascara beneath one of her eyes.

In the corner of his vision, Peter saw Dennis lick his lips.

16

Karaoke had already started at The Coach and Horses as Poppy moved her stuff into the bedsit. She had not, she believed, had much of a choice, ultimately. Victor had, of late, taken to waiting outside her bedroom at the youth hostel, ergo, it was time for her to leave.

Poppy dumped her suitcase on the mattress and tried to work out where to put all her clothes. She was wondering whether she should just leave everything in her suitcase and keep it closed and squeeze it into the tiny space at the end of the bed, when a loud and drunken rendition of 'Alice, Alice, who the fuck is Alice?' started up and wafted in through her window.

Poppy had left it propped open because the air was stale, sour, and damp. The room smelt like a charity shop. Now, she clambered over the mattress to look through the smeared glass. The singing, in one could call it such, was so loud that it sounded as if it was in the street, directly outside. When she peered out, however, she noticed that the street was empty, eerily so almost, the grey concrete dismal and strewn with rubbish. Only something small and scuffling twitched, in the periphery of her vision, near a full rubbish bin, situated to the side of the pub. Through the grubby pub windows, she saw the silhouette of multiple moving shapes.

Poppy felt a wall of lethargy hit then. She slumped, with her back to the window, against the cheap pine headboard. For the first time, a spear of loneliness shot through her. She missed her family and her friends and London.

Poppy tried to give herself a stern talking to. She wouldn't always feel like this, she told herself. University would start, she would meet people and be in lectures all day. She would only ever need to come back to this sad little room, in this sad little street, to sleep.

Hunger eventually roused her and she forced herself to mobilise in order to go in search of a supermarket. By happy coincidence however, as Poppy opened her door, she saw the friendly-looking hippy girl whom she had seen when she was being shown around. The girl was walking up the stairs and smiled widely when she saw Poppy.

"I'm so glad that you decided to take the room, I really hoped you would!" She exclaimed.

Poppy instantly felt much better. The girl introduced herself as Linda and explained that she was doing a Masters in Psychology. There was a maturity to Linda, Poppy would see that quickly as time progressed, in her behaviour and her attitude. She did certainly seem older than Poppy's cohort. At the time, and that afternoon, however, all that Poppy felt was extreme relief that there was somebody friendly living in that weird house with her. Poppy explained her need to buy provisions.

"There's a supermarket nearby that I use. It's not great, but it has the basics. I was just thinking of popping into the Indian buffet place down the road, though, do you fancy it? It's vegetarian and super cheap? They're really friendly, well, I guess I am one of their most loyal customers! What do you think?"

Poppy grinned happily, grabbed her wallet, and followed Linda down the stairs. On the way out, she spotted a tall, skinny boy standing near the stove in the kitchen, framed through the open door.

"That was Jason," Linda explained when they were walking down the street, "He's alright, a bit depressed, studies philosophy and overthinks everything. He has a bigger room and a TV though, so if ever you feel like watching something, just ask him, he doesn't mind."

17

    Simon had noticed, at the end of that interminable church service, that one of the girls was pretty and the other one wasn't, although they were nearly identical. It was funny how that worked. He wondered, still dazed from his light nap, whether the pretty one would be going to school with him and how old she was. There was little time to dwell on that, however, as they moved on and he followed his parents, blinking, into the harsh grey light outside.
    Just outside the church, Robert stood with his puny chest thrust forward and his hands clasped behind his back, looking pompous and somehow smug. He was flanked by a chubby lady in a voluminous flowery frock, her greying hair scrapped up in a tight bun and a young man, very pallid and drawn. One could see Robert in Jacob, but he was a watered down and bleached out version.
    The woman was presumably his wife, Sarah. The remnants of prettiness were there still in the delicate bones of her face, but there were layers of fat in rolls beneath her chin and coating her cheeks, and her lips were set in a thin, unhappy line.
    Everyone exiting the church had to pass the three of them in an awkward procession. It was clear that only Robert enjoyed this routine, his wife and son just looked extremely uncomfortable. The Jensons, bemused by the ceremony of it, joined the line. There didn't seem to be a choice. Once in front of the Pastor's family, Simon noticed that they, the Jensons, were the targets of much curiosity, not just from the pastor and his family, but also from the rest of the congregation. They were all gathered in small, shy huddles in front of the church, their heads lowered, casting surreptitious glances at the newcomers. Simon looked for the two girls with the ballet dancer buns, but they had vanished.
    Robert greeted the family in a formal, semi-disapproving way. It was as if he had studied them and judged them and found them to be wanting. Jacob just nodded his head sombrely but Sarah gave them a seemingly stiff, wobbly smile.
    Bernice raised her eyebrows at Simon once they had walked clear of the procession but Peter scowled at her. They were still being watched. Nobody approached them to greet them however and somewhat

awkwardly the three of them kept walking, feeling the eyes of the assembled crowd burn into their backs until they turned the corner.

"Well, that was fun!" Muttered Simon with heavy sarcasm.

"Tradition is more important to them than fun." Peter shrugged, "That's what tiny communities are like."

"They aren't very friendly." Bernice observed miserably, "I expected them to be more friendly…"

"Yeah," Simon nodded, "Aren't small places supposed to be friendlier than cities? So far, we're not seeing any of that."

"Give it time, they are shy people without great social skills, unused to dealing with outsiders."

"Outsiders! We're hardly aliens!"

"It's early days!" Peter snapped. He was getting tired of cajoling his family. Things were difficult enough for him at the factory without listening to them complain day after day.

That was the day before Peter saw Samantha's backside in her little skirt and he suddenly had something else, something new and exciting to think about.

18

Bernice and Alex always met at the café in the park, although they invariably ended up at his flat. It was a tradition they adhered to right up until the week, nearly a year later, that Bernice moved to Constance with her family. Alex had a lot to say about the move, had a lot to say in general about everything, not much of it positive.

The day the pair had met had been romantic, and the rose-tinted glow persisted in colouring all of Bernice's subsequent meetings with Alex, despite his moods which were as changeable as the weather and veered, sometimes alarmingly, towards cruelty.

There had been a suggestion of a darker side early on, a coldness to his behaviour and his way of speaking to her. It was as if a shutter came down over his friendliness, his cheerful, smiley face, and blocked out the light. But then there was his lovely dog, always there, who seemed to worship Bernice and so, more often than not, she had told herself that she was imagining things, that she was too sensitive, and then she had forgotten about her fears easily as, for months on end, he was warm and solicitous and evidently concerned about her welfare at work. Alex had persuaded Bernice, in fact, to quit her job.

Peter when informed, was surprised.

"I thought you liked teaching?"

"I do like teaching, but there's issues with Ryan and a few of the others, the ex-inmates…I have told you about this before!"

"Yes, but surely that's temporary? They'll move on soon enough and then you will have decent people to teach. I'm just shocked that you would do something so dramatic when it was such a reliable, steady job!"

He had a point, Bernice knew but wouldn't acknowledge it to Peter, or even to herself. She struggled for months to find another job. Alex, initially excited that she'd quit on his suggestion, seemed uninterested in her subsequent and increasingly tedious job search. He even told her that he was bored of listening to her complain about it.

"Our time together is limited," He would comment tersely, "Let's try not to spend it complaining."

That was rich coming from him, Bernice would think, but not say. He complained a great deal about his clients at work, about his colleagues, about a lot of things. Alex complained most of all about Bernice's marriage, although he did not want to marry her himself. He didn't believe in marriage, that is what he repeated time and again.

Bernice would tell him that she was planning on leaving Peter when Simon was eighteen. She had been planning that for some time. In the wee small hours of the night, way before Alex appeared on the scene, Bernice, wide awake, Peter snoring beside her, had acknowledged to herself that what they had, that what her marriage had become, was a friendship merely, and not even a great friendship at that.

Alex would scoff at that.

"Why wait until Simon is eighteen?" He would say. And he had a point, of sorts.

"It is not some magic number. He will not suddenly stop caring if his parents separate!"

Alex believed that Bernice should leave Peter then and there. Within two months of meeting, he was already hounding her about it. To leave Peter and to move in with him. "A chance of happiness." He would reiterate, although Bernice was not always happy with Alex, often she would feel nervous and insecure, as if she was not good enough. In the empty cold space of his flat, a loneliness would besiege her, a new sort of loneliness. Especially in the long hours of the forbidden afternoons with Alex snoring oblivious beside her and the dog asleep in the next room.

But Bernice had done this to herself, she knew that.

She had learnt, early on, to bite her tongue when Alex ranted about marriage, or indeed anything. They only met once a week, after all. He was right that they should make the most of their time together. After spending hours with Alex, Peter would seem even more placid and indifferent than he usually did. Alex seemed to watch Bernice's every move and yet Peter seemed to barely notice her existence, so preoccupied was he by work and then the pending relocation and new factory.

It was in March, six months before the move, that Bernice finally managed to get a job as a special needs teaching assistant in a local primary school. It was a difficult job, the pay was terrible and the child she was tasked with looking after had a tendency towards unexpected violent outbursts. Alex was clearly uninterested in hearing about it though, and Peter told her it was her own fault for leaving her previous job.

19

The bedrooms in the cottage in Constance were, objectively, not so bad. There were two full-sized doubles and a single. They all had the twee, cutesy sloping ceiling going on though. Bernice didn't mind it. Simon, with his long, gangly limbs, hated it. He kept hitting his head, it just added to his permanent state of irritation.

There were only a few days left until school started, and his uniform hung on his wardrobe door, brand new and taunting him. The wardrobe itself was narrow and already filled to the brim with his other, casual clothes. The uniform, with its stiff, bulky material, didn't fit. Simon felt it as a dark presence there, glowering at him, as he lay in his bed, (at least that was of a decent size), staring moodily at the slopping ceiling. A tiny damp patch in the shape of a rabbit, or a large-eared dog hovered directly above him.

As a family, they had collectively decided to skip a week of church, despite the supposed potential for socialisation, because all three of them admitted that they had found it depressing, which somehow seemed to defeat the purpose. Nevertheless, Simon, lying there in the cosy cocoon of his bedroom, would have relished the prospect of seeing the girl with the ballet dancer's bun again. She was literally the only potential positive of life in Constance that he could think of, and he thought about her often, the way her face appeared before him as he had roused himself from his light snooze; her eyes wide and blue and startled or amused. (Although that may have been a trick of the light or of his imagination.)

To get to the high school in Tensit, the kids in Constance took the same village bus that Peter would occasionally take to the factory when he did not have access to the family car. The bus turned off, down a narrow country road, before it reached the factory and trundled towards Tensit, past a couple of other hamlets, too miniscule to even be referred to as villages, to collect other children.

During term time, that bus, normally nearly empty, was full to the brim just before school started and just after it finished. It only ran every half an hour and the journey from Constance to the high school, with all the stops, took forty-five minutes, so if one missed the 8am bus, one was very late and, as per school rules, got a detention.

Just before 8am on the first day of term, therefore, Simon in his stiff (and supremely uncomfortable) school uniform, hovered self-consciously at the bus stop along with more than twenty other teenagers, all stuffed into the same unattractive garments. Many of them were much younger and their uniforms mostly swamped them. The coarse scratchy material would have to wait years to be stuffed with the right amount of flesh and bone and muscle, by which time they would be shiny and bedraggled and worn. They all wore trousers, both girls and boys and Simon was thinking vaguely how progressive that was, when he spotted the girl with the ballet bun and her sister.

They were both leaning on a nearby low wall and huddled together, not talking to anyone else. Their hair was pulled back in tight buns as before, and their skinny, pale necks looked even more pitifully vulnerable emerging from the harsh ugliness of the school blazer. There were several other kids in the way and Simon, naturally, could not make it obvious that he was staring at them, so he scrutinised them via a series of rapid glances. Even leaning on the wall, although very similar, and although both girls were facing downwards, it was still apparent that one girl was taller than the other. That was the one with the pretty face, Simon knew, the one that he fancied.

As nonchalantly as possible, Simon manoeuvred himself closer to them, so that he could be near to them on the bus.

20

Poppy was extremely happy that she had met Linda, and even happier that they were living in the same house. Linda, in fact, was literally one of the only good things about that residence.

The building was home to numerous odours, none of them pleasant. There was a ubiquitous and all-pervasive smell of damp, which intermingled occasionally throughout the days with a truly foul stench of drains, mostly in the bathroom and the kitchen. Jason, a pleasant but taciturn boy would nod morosely and mumble gloomily about pipes.

"Has anyone tried talking to the landlord?" Asked Poppy, exasperated and disgusted but already predicting the answer to her question.

Linda smiled and sighed, "Oh yes, several times, he just says that it's because the building is old."

"But that's nonsense!"

"Yes, yes, it is, but he won't listen to reason, and, as you can probably tell, he's not the easiest and most friendly bloke to chat to!"

That much was true. Poppy had seen very little of him since moving in, fortunately, but she had to walk past the shop on a daily basis to get to campus, and often he would be behind the counter inside, the silhouette of a man, and she would sense, rather than see, his eyes trailing after her and she would picture very clearly their cold, empty stare.

Lectures had started, after a freshers' week during which Poppy attended various club nights and fairs with Linda, who had obviously done it all before, but was more than happy to do it again with Poppy. Poppy was hugely relieved, she would have felt nervous and self-conscious turning up at those events alone. Poppy could be sociable when she had to be, but Linda was one of those people for whom being happy and friendly to everyone was second nature. If Poppy hadn't liked her so much, she would have been jealous. As it was, Poppy was encompassed in the glow of Linda's personality, so that a kind of secondary light shone also on her.

By the time she started her lectures, therefore, Poppy found that she knew a surprising amount of people, even just to say hello to, at least. At her very first, introductory, lecture, she sat next to a girl she hadn't seen before and introduced herself.

It very soon became obvious that the girl, Maisie, was very quiet, nothing like Linda. Poppy found, however, that she herself, in the presence of Maisie, became far more outgoing, an extrovert almost. It was as if she was channelling her inner Linda.

Maisie had pale beige hair, thin and wavy about her small face. Her eyes were large and brown and watchful and she was not given to smiling. There was an intensity and intelligence, Poppy fancied, about Maisie's serious gaze. Maisie lived in catered halls of campus and she would frequently take Poppy back with her, after lectures, and share her lunch. It was carb-heavy and quite tasteless. Poppy would often joke that it was like prison food, but would demolish it hungrily all the same.

"Can I see where you live?" Maisie asked one day. She had heard all about the bedsit, and yet Poppy was somehow reluctant to bring her back there, and specifically to introduce her to Linda. It certainly wasn't because the bedsit was decrepit, the halls were extremely shabby too. It was because Poppy wanted to keep her two friends separate, but she couldn't articulate why. She couldn't have explained the fact of it, even to herself.

21

Since moving to Constance, Bernice had not heard from Alex. He owned a mobile phone but Bernice did not. Peter was the only one in their household to possess one as he needed it for work. Still, the cottage in Constance had a landline, and before moving there, Bernice had told Alex the number. He had responded to the information at the time, Bernice recalled, in, what had become, throughout the year they had been together, his trademark, increasingly stroppy manner.

"Why would I need that? I can't call you there, it would seem suspicious, what would be the point?"

His rejoinder made little sense, as he had had no qualms whatsoever in calling the landline when they were both in London. He hadn't worried about it being suspicious then. The difference being, of course, that now he couldn't see Bernice every week anymore. Now that he could no longer sleep with her, he had lost interest. That was how it seemed. Alex had made note of the new number all the same, but he was not calling it. Bernice had always been in possession of his mobile number too, obviously, but she summoned up the last vestiges of her self-esteem and resisted calling. Six months previously, fully embroiled in the heady throes of their affair, she would have called his number in a heartbeat. Yet now, from a distance, a worm of doubt had somehow crawled in. It was a relief, strangely now, to be faced with the solid, almost comforting wall of Peter's unwavering indifference, rather than be grappling with the chronic insecurity which her affair with Alex had gradually induced.

Somehow, and by very gradual degrees he had made Bernice doubt herself. He had made her more anxious than she already was to start with. Because he had started off so charming, she had struggled to recognise his behaviour for what it was. Bernice had been reluctant to let go of her romantic interpretation of that initial encounter in the park. The memory of it had sustained her for so long; it was like a comfort blanket. To admit to herself that it was tarnished from the start, a deluded fairytale constructed from a duplicitous act or a manipulation, was almost unbearable.

Yet, in the cold light of day, she would have to admit to herself, that ever since the charm offensive of that first meeting, the relationship had gone downhill, via gradual increments. There was the endless grumpiness certainly, but there was also the casual, matter-of-fact putdowns about Bernice's appearance or somehow her potential or lack thereof.

"You are middle-aged now." He would say, "You're not going to achieve anything much anymore, that ship has sailed." Or: "You don't look too bad for your age, I've seen women who look worse."

If she reacted at all, or showed displeasure, he would claim that it was speaking in jest, that she was too sensitive to take a joke. Yet if she dared to say anything similar back to him, (she had only tried once), he would go mad.

Without him, in Constance, sleepless next to Peter snoring heavily next to her, she began to wonder if Alex had targeted her from the start. He could have gone for a younger, more attractive lady, but no. He had gone for an ordinary-looking middle-aged woman. Was that deliberate, Bernice wondered? Had he gone for someone younger and prettier with their self-esteem intact, they may have been more able to defend themselves.

That wasn't the only thing that niggled at Bernice however. When the Jensons had left London, they had handed the keys to their house over to a local estate agent hoping that they would be able to rent it out whilst they were staying in Constance. The agent had just informed them that the boiler had several significant issues and the house was suffering from potential subsidence, and both problems meant that the house was unrentable.

"Potential subsidence?" Bernice had all but shrieked over the phone. "What does that even mean?"

"There is a huge crack in the kitchen wall, just behind the fridge, had you not noticed?"

Bernice had not. She had not had cause to look behind the fridge since they had bought it many years ago, and wondered why the estate agent had thought to do so.

"What can we do?" She asked him then, a bit desperately. The family had been relying on that rent money to boost their income. Both Peter and Bernice had significant credit card debt.

"Nothing." Responded the man curtly. "It all needs looking into and fixing, and it won't be cheap. Until you get that done, I'm afraid we can't possibly put it on the market."

22

Just before Simon managed to lower himself into the seat behind the two sisters on the bus, he was jostled out of the way by a small but rowdy group of boys.

"Out of the way, new boy! That seat is ours!"

Simon was gripped suddenly by the arm and physically manoeuvred back into the aisle.

"OY!" The bus driver, a rotund man, turned to glare at them, "Behave yourselves!" His tone was angry but also resigned. It didn't seem as if he would actually do anything about their behaviour. Probably, he could not be bothered to get up. The two girls with the ballet dancers' buns turned at the ruckus, and the older one scowled.

"Give it a rest, will you Gary!" She directed this at one of the boys, a dark-haired one, who snorted in derision.

"Careful, Princess Emily has spoken, boys, we better behave ourselves!"

Emily, thought Simon, that was her name. Emily muttered something under her breath and turned to stare out of the window as the monotonous verdant landscape unfurled. Her younger sister drew her arms tightly around herself and her school bag which was in her lap. Both of them were thin and fragile-looking, insubstantial somehow.

Simon, simultaneously exhilarated and exhausted, could feel a bruise already smarting and aching on his upper arm, beneath his jacket. In the aisle still, he cast surreptitious glances at Emily and watched the boys and wondered how come he had not come across them in Constance before. Three of the group had piled into the seat that he had been dragged from, and as he observed them and the miles trundled passed, Simon realised that he had, in fact, seen them before, only they had looked very different. He had seen them clad in weirdly formal old-fashioned outfits in church that day, the same morning when he had spotted Emily. Here, on the bus, they looked ordinary again. Not as fashionable as London kids, no, but the uniform was a great equaliser and their hair was normal, at least. They didn't seem friendly or kindly unfortunately, that much was obvious. It was a shame, because Simon knew he needed friends, not least to appease his curiosity about the weird church, for one.

The bus stopped exactly in front of the high school. It looked much smaller than Simon's old school in London, but had clearly been built during the same unimaginative, utilitarian era. It was a rectangle of ugly grey brick and the weak sun reflected in the endless windows which provided a view of the staff carpark, and then off to the side a netball court, and behind that a field. The school grounds were surrounded by the village of Tensit. It appeared to sit bang in the middle, like the body of a spider. Around it, terraced houses lined up in rows interspersed by concrete council blocks. Further out there were more expensive homes, some farms.

The kids poured out of the bus and into the wide main doorway of the school, chattering and shouting. Even though there were far fewer kids than at his school in London, the strangeness of it all threatened to overwhelm Simon. He had stopped just outside the entrance to take a breath, when he heard a soft voice just beside him. There was a fragrance, suddenly; soap and vanilla.

"Are you OK?" Asked Emily.

23

Peter was convinced, within days, that there was something going on between Dennis and Samantha. Initially, he had presumed that it was only within the realms of Dennis's lewd imagination, but there was definitely an atmosphere when the two of them were in the same room together, a tension.

Still, Peter was far too busy to dwell on what his colleagues were getting up to, and beyond a tiny stab of disappointment, he didn't think about it. He had much bigger problems. Whilst the factory was equipped with sparkling, brand new machines; some of them were the wrong ones and had to be replaced. Work could not start until the new machines arrived as they were an essential component in the production line, therefore everything was delayed and Peter's company was losing money by the minute.

Although the oversight in the machine order had not been Peter's fault, (some secretary had copied something down wrong somewhere along the line,) blame had to be allocated and the buck now stopped with him.

Peter's boss called from London multiple times a day asking for updates. As nothing could happen without the new machines, and delivery would take at least two days, those phone calls were increasingly tense. Peter would have loved to ignore those calls, but of course, he couldn't. He realised that his hands had involuntarily started trembling every time he lifted his phone to his ear.

In the office, which he shared with Dennis, he noticed Dennis stare at his hands with an expression which somehow combined both disgust and glee. He must, thought Peter, think that he, Peter, was weak and pathetic. Dennis was exactly the type of neanderthal to think that empathy and emotions were 'woke.'

Samantha had her own small office just outside Peter's. It was more of a thoroughfare with a desk really, in that everyone had to get past Samantha in order to get to Peter. Not that she ever stopped anyone from accessing him. Samantha's very proximity, however, did mean that, fortunately, Peter was often relieved of the presence of Dennis, as he seemed to spend most of his time leaning over Samantha's desk. Peter kept his door shut, so that all he could discern was a low murmur. He was too preoccupied to think about either of them for more than a second until the right machines arrived at the factory.

On the afternoon that they did eventually arrive, a full day after they were supposed to, Peter watched from his window, as the huge lorries pulled into the loading bay of the factory. He was unpleasantly surprised to realise that his skin, under his clothes, felt prickly. The reason, as he quickly discerned, was that he was slick with cold sweat.

As if that discovery wasn't troubling enough, at that very moment, whilst he was still standing at the window, staring unseeing at the huge lorry, he heard what could only be described as a piercing shriek from directly behind him, from the room where Samantha was based.

Peter's heart gave an uncomfortable jolt, he felt it. For one tiny second, he wondered whether he would feel the same jolt just before he died. What fresh hell is this? The words came to him unbidden, and then, distractedly, he wondered who had said that originally, before turning around and striding towards Samantha's room in a hurry.

24

Poppy was so busy with her new lectures and hanging out with Linda and Maisie that she had almost forgotten that her old, albeit not particularly close, friend from school, Tina, was also starting Nottingham University.

They bumped into each other by accident as Poppy and Linda were taking a walk through the gorgeous campus. It was a sparkling autumn day with a translucent clear sky and a light frost had already rendered the grass crispy underfoot. Poppy and Linda were bundled up against the brisk wind in a selection of colourful scarves. They had just crossed some stepping stones over a fast-moving stream when Poppy saw a diminutive scurrying figure before them, walking on a parallel path. She was hunched over with her head down.

It took Poppy longer than it should have done to realise that the figure was Tina. She seemed, in that second, extremely unfamiliar, as if she were an actor you remember having seen somewhere, but can't recollect exactly where.

It was a sense of politeness and duty, more than anything else, which compelled Poppy to rush towards Tina then and greet her.

"How great to see you! Where have you been? Weren't you here during Freshers? I'm sure we would have bumped into each other!"

Linda hung back, and Tina glanced at her, almost anxiously. She looked serious and drawn.

"I…well, I had some family issues." She glanced at Linda again, as if she didn't want to say too much in front of a stranger. "I had to skip Freshers unfortunately. I just arrived on the first day of lectures."

"Oh, bummer." Poppy didn't quite know what to say. She made her own expression more sombre. "Did you get good halls at least?"

"Oh, yeah, I organised that ages ago, so that wasn't an issue. Nottingham was my first choice."

She said that in a dismissive way, as if it was unimportant.

"Lucky!" Said Poppy, "I had to find my own accommodation."

"Oy!" laughed Linda, finally joining in. She wasn't the sort of person who would stay in the background of a conversation for long.

"If you hadn't had to find your own accommodation, you would never have met me!"

"That's true I suppose!"

Tina was obviously trying to smile along with them, but it came across as fake, more of a grimace. Somewhat awkwardly, Poppy and Tina exchanged numbers and promised to catch up soon. To Poppy then, at that time, it almost felt like a chore that she was obliged to carry out.

On another day, when Poppy and Linda were in the centre of town shopping at a budget supermarket, popular amongst students, Poppy spotted Victor walking ahead of them. His spindly black-clad legs and distinctive goth hair made him stand out, even in a town full of students. From a distance he looked small and pathetic. Poppy could not believe that he had ever had the power to make her feel uneasy. Or, before that, briefly, that she had felt any kind of bond with him. It was embarrassing to think about, there, in the sunlight, with her new best friend, Linda.

Somewhat inexplicably, she pointed Victor out to Linda, who laughed. Poppy had not thought that Linda was ever mean and she was surprised at the things that she said about Victor then, the derogatory comments that she made were even slightly shocking. Quickly, she recalled, however, that she had already said unkind things about Victor to Linda, and Linda was merely echoing them back to her.

25

    Emily walked next to Simon as they made their way into class. They did not speak beyond establishing that they both lived in Constance. Her voice, when she spoke, was soft and low. The high school was so small that there was only one class per year group. Happily, it transpired that Emily was fifteen, like Simon and they were, therefore, in the same class.
    Simon was so chuffed with this discovery that he barely paid any attention to anything else about the school until they were sitting down in their form room, to which he had been led by Emily. She sat near the front of the class and so did he, in the desk next to hers. If someone moved him then so be it, but he thought he may as well give it a go.
    It was then that he spotted the three boys from Constance who had pulled him out of his seat on the bus. Unfortunately, they seemed to be in that class too. The one called Gary spotted Simon, nudged his friend and the two of them smirked nastily. Unsurprisingly, all three were seated in the back row, presumably, as they were all loitering there as if they belonged.
    Simon sighed heavily. It seemed as if he had already made enemies without even trying. So much for the 'cool kid from London' theory, as espoused by his mother. All he needed now was the rough-looking kids that were slouching outside the department store in Cavershall to show up.
    Emily, good deed completed, was ignoring Simon then and chatting to a small group of friends. Simon, to avoid staring at her gormlessly, looked around the room. It wasn't interesting. The room resembled any other classroom anywhere. It had the same peeling notices pinned on the walls, beseeching the kids to adhere to the same rules, the same worn and grubby thin industrial carpet, the same smell of cheap aftershave, urine and sweat with an undertone of cabbage from the canteen, the same desks with the same graffiti etched deeply into the cheap pale wood.
    Simon felt a great sense of doom as he contemplated his immediate environment, and he was just calculating exactly how many days he needed to spend there, when an adult, presumably a teacher, walked into the room. She was a tall, angular woman with her long dark brown hair pulled into a high pony tail. Plain glasses with cheap black frames perched on her bony nose. Her skin was warmly tanned and her eyes, her

best feature, were wide and brown and expressive. She could have been any age between twenty-five and forty, Simon found it impossible to judge.

The woman stood before the white board and introduced herself in a lilting voice as Miss Sanchez. Her smile was wide and she looked kindly. She was new to Simon obviously, but clearly, she was new to the rest of the kids too, as a low chattering hum could be heard almost immediately and Simon could discern many exclamations of surprise.

"Miss! Miss! What happened to Mr. Jolly?"

"Is Mr. Jolly sick miss? Has he left?"

"Did he get sacked, Miss, is that what happened?" That comment was from the back row.

Simon was very relieved to note that all the desks were occupied by then, but the rough-looking boys he had spotted in Cavershall were nowhere to be seen. They must, he reasoned happily, be in another class, or maybe even in another school or too old for school entirely, although that seemed too much to hope for.

Miss Sanchez, with admirable patience, explained that Mr. Jolly had moved to another part of England and to another job, and no, he had not been sacked, but moved of his own volition. Eventually, they all settled down and the tedious administrative tasks, ubiquitous on all first days back, began.

26

Bernice, of course, did not have a job in Constance. Although, she had not loved her last two jobs, they had provided her day with a structure that was welcome, as well as a wage of course. Without a rigid timetable, imposed by someone else, Bernice realised that she was floundering. Up until Simon's new school had started, at least she could hang out with him and the two of them would spend their time slouching at the kitchen table and complaining about Constance. There was a lot to say. Simon's presence, even taciturn, had distracted Bernice from thinking about Alex, and how he had seemingly forgotten about her entirely.

She started questioning, alone there in the claustrophobic silent kitchen, on the very first morning that Simon went to school, what her purpose was now? What was she supposed to do with herself, now that her kids barely needed her, she didn't have a job and her husband seemed wholly indifferent to her existence?

Bored and restless, Bernice took to going for long walks through the tiny village and down the paths alongside the fields that surrounded Constance. Sometimes, she would meet dog walkers or, more occasionally, people walking alone, and she would greet them. Mostly, they would greet her back, not in a particularly enthusiastic manner. Only on one occasion did a man ignore her completely, which felt, somehow, particularly galling.

She wondered whether she should get a dog. It would give her a legitimate excuse for those lonely walks, although she had never thought of herself as much of a 'dog person,' not until she had met Alex's dog, that was. She missed Alex's dog almost more than she missed him. Or maybe she didn't miss him at all, just the idea of him. In particular, the rose-tinted version of him that had been presented to her on that first day they met, and which had been deteriorating ever since, like mildew forming over a once beautiful painting, or some kind of fungus.

She was walking through the village one morning when she almost literally bumped into Sarah, Robert's wife, who was just emerging from the village shop with laden bags. Bernice had glimpsed Sarah from a distance several times, but Sarah had always had her head lowered, and had not looked as if she wanted to stop for a chat. Also, Bernice felt a bit guilty that they had not made it back to church.

Sarah didn't particularly look like she wanted to stop for a chat then either. She looked tired and drawn in the harsh white daylight, her pallid skin blotchy and somehow greyish. She looked at Bernice who was right in front of her and jolted in surprise. She smiled but it was clearly false. Her teeth were yellowish and there was an obvious black gap quite near the front.

"You're the mother, aren't you?" She said abruptly then, but in a quiet voice. "The mother of the new family that's just arrived, I mean?"

Bernice nodded, a bit taken aback.

"I don't think that's been my main label since the kids were in primary school!" She smiled.

"What would you consider your main label then?" Sarah regarded her curiously.

"I don't really know, I… haven't really thought about it!" She knew she sounded flustered. This wasn't what she, Bernice, thought small talk was, and she was unprepared.

"I guess," admitted Bernice finally, "I am finding myself at a bit of a loose end. I mean, I don't have a job here and my kids, well, my son who is still living with us here, he is independent now so…"

"You know, I can always use extra help in the church with admin, cleaning, taking care of the flowers and so forth?"

As Sarah spoke her voice got louder, her tone more confident, and enthusiastic.

"I would love to have you!"

Bernice shuddered inwardly. The memory of the tedious church service they had attended was still fresh in her mind along with the closed-off, unfriendly faces of the parishioners.

"I'm actually just…" She floundered desperately, she couldn't think of an excuse, of anything concrete she could actually be doing, rather than just going for a walk, which was the truth of it.

"I'm going there right now!" Declared Sarah, all bustling and confident now that Bernice had been ensnared, "I was just buying cleaning supplies and snacks for the youth group which Jacob is starting. Why don't you come with me and we can have a chat?"

27

It took Peter but two seconds to swing open the door of his office and stand in front of Samantha's desk. She was sitting ramrod straight and staring ahead of her, almost as if hypnotised or in severe shock. She looked unnaturally pale, even under all the make-up, and Peter panicked that she might faint.

"What's wrong? Are you OK? Why did you scream?" The questions poured out of Peter. He found himself to be quite breathless.

"I...I stubbed my toe, it...hurt, I was surprised, that's all, sorry for squealing like that!"

She sighed deeply and lowered her eyes to look down at her untidy desk. Everything was usually lined up very neatly, but just then there were papers and notes scattered everywhere, as if a projectile had landed in the middle of the desk. She was avoiding eye contact with Peter, that much was obvious. But why? He didn't believe her for one instance, but he could hardly force her to tell him the real reason she had shrieked.

They both remained as they were in an awkward tableau as the seconds passed. There was more colour in her face then, that was a relief to him. Something niggled at him though, not exactly an idea, more a fraction of a thought. Where was Dennis? He had been there earlier; Peter was sure he had heard his annoying voice through the door of the office.

"Where is Dennis?" He asked then, genuinely curious.

Samantha's head jolted up and a pinkish flush, not unbecoming, suffused her neck and her cheeks.

Aha, thought Peter. The shriek had been something to do with Dennis, but what exactly?

"I don't know where he is." She responded in a small, unhappy voice.

"He was here earlier, though?"

"Yes." She drew her lips firmly together. It was clear that Peter was not going to get any more information from her. He stood there, rocking on his heels anyway though. He felt somehow responsible for Samantha, for her wellbeing. He thought of his own daughter alone in a different part of the UK. Samantha was not that much older than Poppy. Very different though, yes. He felt another strange jolt in his heart as he thought of Poppy with her dyed hair and black chunky boots, excessive eyeliner, and attitude.

"Right, yes." The silence was spreading uncomfortably around the pair of them.

"Well, let me know if you need anything." Said Peter, knowing that he sounded feeble. With that, he turned and went back into his office and shut the door. He found himself struggling to focus on his work however. He went to look out of the window but the huge lorry had gone. At least the machines had been delivered and work could hopefully start the following day. Peter tried to sit at his desk and deal with his copious paperwork but he felt distracted and twitchy. Dennis did not return to the office.

The nights had started to draw in earlier, by gradual degrees and the evenings, in particular, seemed to fall dramatically in the countryside, like a heavy curtain blacking out the sky. There were no nearby buildings, no streetlights, just the stars, on a clear night at least.

By six, when the administrative part of the factory officially stopped work, the sky had already dimmed to a murky grey; heavy rain clouds added to the impression that winter was imminent.

Dissatisfied that he had not achieved much that afternoon, and puzzled as to where Dennis might be, Peter was on his way out when he realised that Samantha was still there, sitting exactly as he had left her, only now her desk was neat again. She was typing. "How do you get home, Samantha?"

He had asked the question without thinking about it. It had risen up in him and emerged unbidden. He knew anyway. She got the bus back and forth to Tensit, the same bus that took Simon to school. She looked up, startled, and in the same small voice as before, confirmed what Peter already knew.

"It looks like heavy rain, how about I give you a lift?" He asked.

28

Linda did not like Poppy to go out with other people in the evening.

The strange fact of this did not become clear until several weeks later when Maisie and Tina both asked Poppy to go to the pub in the evening with their respective housemates, on separate occasions. Until then, Poppy had spent all her evenings with Linda. After the organised excitement of Freshers' week, they had not done much. Mainly Poppy had hung out in Linda's room which was bigger than her own, or sometimes they both hung out in Jason's room and watched TV. They had a good laugh and they always got on, but by the time that Maisie and Tina asked Poppy to go out with them, Poppy was ready to broaden her social circle and to see a bit more of other students and the Nottingham pub scene. Even though Linda knew a great many people, she didn't seem to want to socialise or even be invited out.

Linda pulled a strange face when Poppy told her she was going out with Maisie and her housemates.

"Why would you do that?" She asked.

"What do you mean?" Asked Poppy confused.

"Why would you go out with other people when we have a good time together? What am I supposed to do when you are out?" "Erm, I don't know…go out with your own friends?" Poppy couldn't quite believe the way the conversation was going. She was half-thinking that it must be a joke. Suddenly it came to her, however, almost in a flash; Linda didn't seem to have any actual friends! Poppy was incredulous, she almost couldn't believe the discovery that she had just made and yet, it was true. Suddenly, it was obvious. The entire time that she had known Linda, over two weeks by then, Linda had mentioned no other friends, seen no other friends. And why was someone who had spent over three years in Nottingham, (Linda had done her graduate degree there too), friendless here in this bedsit?

Why wasn't she living with, or at least hanging out with, friends that she had met here in Nottingham? That would be 'normal,' wouldn't it? Yes, she seemed to know everyone, but it was only on a very superficial basis.

There was a loaded silence between them, which there never had been before, and within it, Poppy felt herself floundering. Suddenly, and miserably, she saw Linda in a completely different light. She had seemed to be a solid friend, bestie material, and yet now this new possessiveness was making her highly unappealing, almost repulsive in a way. This had been the exact same reason that Poppy had wanted to get away from Victor's scrutiny in the Youth Hostel, she absolutely did not want to be monitored and controlled by anybody. Poppy knew she had to put her foot down before whatever this was escalated.

"I don't want to see anybody else, I want to hang out with you." Said Linda then, her face wearing an unappealing petulant expression.

"Well, I'm sorry," Stated Poppy as firmly as she could, still feeling incredulous that it had come to this. "Maybe you should widen your own circle a little bit and socialise more. I know that you know a lot of people to talk to, maybe go out with one of them? I, myself, am going out with Maisie and her housemates."

"Well, you're not the person I thought you were then." Sniffed Linda in a dramatic manner and flounced out.

It was Saturday afternoon and they had been arguing in the kitchen. It smelt damp and disgusting as it always did. Karaoke had just started up at the pub and the distant roar of drunk caterwauling thundered through the walls.

Poppy, alone afterwards in the kitchen, sighed deeply to herself. It was possible, she realised suddenly, that she had made a huge mistake in moving to this bedsit and befriending Linda.

29

It was a tough gig for Miss Sanchez. Simon realised this almost immediately and felt sorry for her. The class was disruptive and there was a cold veneer to them. They were not warm-hearted, kind people. He felt this quite strongly, and yet he wasn't sure exactly why, it was more an overall impression, or an aura, even.

There had certainly been rough elements in his class in London, and even more in his school, obviously, but it wasn't that, or not just that. There was a lack of empathy about this cohort, a lack of feeling, and unlike his classmates in London, this lot all seemed the same. In London, you would get some who were brutish and deliberately mean, others who were indifferent and then a small, but significant group who went out of their way to be kind and inclusive.

Simon could not discern any of those people here. No one was kind or inclusive, not to him, nor to Miss Sanchez. They were all either indifferent or downright rude.

Even Emily, for whom he had had high hopes, (for whom he still had high hopes, truth be told, because Simon still fancied her), even she had ignored him completely after depositing him graciously in the classroom on that first morning.

Miss Sanchez, like Simon himself, was an outsider and he watched her try and control her class with a steady authoritative tone, with the air of an actress who has stoically learnt her lines. He then heard her stammer and saw her hand shake as she gave out slips of paper, and he watched as her determinedly optimistic mask slipped and her mouth drooped at the edges and her lips trembled.

The class had listened to her for maybe fifteen minutes and then started fidgeting and acting as if she didn't exist. They chatted and put their feet up on seats and shouted at each other across the room. One of the boys was chucking a tennis ball around, it bounced off the walls and the desks and things fell to the ground.

"Please stop!" Implored Miss Sanchez, still trying to use a firm voice, but they ignored her.

Bounce, bounce went the tennis ball.

Another boy started flying paper aeroplanes.

Even the sensible-looking girls, and Simon would have thought Emily was one of them, ignored her completely and chatted to each other, very much as if there was no teacher in the room at all. Simon found it astounding. He, himself, tried to catch Miss Sanchez's eye to communicate solidarity and pity, but after half an hour of that behaviour, she no longer looked at any of them. She sat at the desk and kept her head lowered.

"What are we supposed to be doing?" Simon literally patted Emily on the shoulder. Emily looked startled to be interrupted in her chatting and shrugged.

"Who knows?"

"Don't you think we should be listening to her?"

Emily looked incredulous, as if Simon had suggested something totally bizarre.

"She's the teacher, it's her job to make us listen!" Emily scoffed. Her face, which had seemed pretty and kindly to Simon not long ago, assumed a closed, mean expression. She was less attractive, in that instance, for sure.

For an hour, the chaos continued, and close to the end of that time, Miss Sanchez wrote a list on the board. There were two columns. A and B and their names were all written in one or the other.

Miss Sanchez stood and raised her voice until it was literally a shout.

"This is your GCSE year, it is important. You will be in different groups for some subjects; Maths, Science and English. I have different timetables on my desk for you depending on whether you are A or B. Come and get them on your way to Maths. That's what you've got now. You can all go."

She sounded resigned somehow, hopeless. Simon tried to smile at her still, but she wouldn't look at him. He was in the 'A' list. He wondered if that meant he was stupid or slightly less stupid.

30

The church, empty of people, seemed enormous and echoey. It looked clean, but also had the same slightly damp, stale smell as all communal halls, and dust motes floated abundantly in the air.

Sarah bustled down the central aisle with her carrier bags. Bernice had offered to take one from her but she had declined. Bernice followed in her wake, sceptical still, but relieved all the same to have something to do. Boredom was a killer, who knew?

"We'll keep this stuff in the kitchen for now." Declared Sarah. "You can help me put it away."

"You mentioned Jacob is starting a youth group?" Bernice asked with polite interest.

"Yes, on a Friday early evening. He's just graduated, you know, and won't be taking over from Robert for a good many years, but obviously he can still be involved in various church activities. He should be involved, in fact!"

They were in the kitchen of the church, a cramped, poorly ventilated space which had its own unpleasant odour; fetid, poorly washed tea towels, the ubiquitous damp. There was one tiny oblong window just underneath the ceiling. It was closed. One would need a chair or a ladder to reach it. The sink had clearly been white at some point in the distant past but was now stained a curious and disgusting shade of yellow. The fake-wood work surfaces fostered, in their corners, black specks of mould.

"Isn't the ghost supposed to be in here somewhere?" asked Bernice in a jokey tone, thinking to herself that any self- respecting ghost could surely find itself a more pleasant environment to haunt.

Sarah snorted. "You don't want to believe all that nonsense. People round here sometimes have nothing better to do then make things up!"

Bernice wondered to herself why Robert had recounted the story then, was it just a device to get them interested in the church?

The supplies for the youth club, would not have appealed to any youth that Bernice had ever come across, certainly not to her own children. There was the cheapest orange squash, plain cut-price biscuits, pink wafers, a packet of custard creams and a jumbo packet of ready salted crisps. She put the snacks away in the cupboards that were indicated to her without comment.

"You can help me sweep the floor now, if you don't mind." Sarah declared. She was sounding much more confident and bossier now than when she had met Bernice outside. It wasn't even a question, more of a demand. Perhaps, Sarah felt more sure of herself inside the church as it was her domain.

"We have an on-going fight against dust and dirt here, all the people traipsing in and out, of course, it's inevitable."

"Do you have more than one service a week then?"

"Oh yes, we have a full service on Wednesday evenings and prayer groups on Tuesdays and Thursday evenings, you should come along!"

Sarah turned to face Bernice across the rows of grey plastic chairs. They were both holding old-fashioned brooms which were largely ineffectual against the dust. Mostly they just pushed it up into the air where dust clouds formed and floated in a leisurely fashion. They had been at it for half an hour by then and Bernice had had enough. She didn't mind helping out, but sweeping with these useless brooms was pointless. Pointless and boring. Going for a walk by herself was suddenly looking much more appealing. Also, she definitely didn't want to get sucked into coming here regularly.

"Maybe." She said to Sarah, nodding in a non-committal way, and then just for something to say, "Are they popular these services? Do many people go?"

"More and more people." Said Sarah firmly, "Well, it's a small community, of course, it's never going to attract hordes of people, but I have high hopes for Jacob's youth club on a Friday, there is very little for young people to do here in the village. You should persuade your Simon to go!"

31

Samantha's perfume was flowery and overpowering within the limited confines of Peter's car. It was strange, he thought, how he had not noticed it at all in the office. No doubt that was because it competed ineffectually there with the strong chemical odours drifting up from the machines on the factory floor.

Samantha arranged herself tidily on the passenger seat, with her small hands folded over her handbag in her lap. Peter, even without looking at her, felt a jolt of excitement, of lust. It had a lot to do with being in such proximity and being completely alone with her.

"Off we go to Tensit then!" Peter chuckled feebly and then winced at his own attempt at jollity.

Samantha, next to him, said nothing.

"Do you live by yourself?" He asked, unable to keep the hope out of his tone.

"I have a flatmate, a girl I went to college with." Said Samantha.

"You went to college?" asked Peter surprised.

"Just secretarial." She snorted, emitting a short, surprisingly bitter laugh. "No university for the likes of me!"

Peter didn't know what to say to that. He had never seen this less-than-perky side to her, she certainly didn't reveal it at work. He wondered if he should be flattered that she felt she could be her true self in front of him.

"University is not for everyone." He said then, in what he considered a soothing tone.

"It is for everyone who wants to get away from here." Retorted Samantha.

"Do you want to get away from here?"

"I didn't before. I used to think it was fine, but lately, I've been thinking…" She glanced over at Peter then as if suddenly remembering that he was her boss and she should be careful what she revealed about herself.

"Not that I don't appreciate the job, you understand, it's a great job, a brilliant opportunity! My mate, the girl I live with, she's working in a mechanic's reception. She hates it."

"I'm very glad you don't hate your job." Said Peter, keeping to the same soothing tone. "I wouldn't want you to be unhappy, well, I wouldn't want anyone to be unhappy."

"*You* have never made me unhappy!"

Peter heard the stress and picked up on it immediately.

"If not me, then who?" He asked quickly.

"No one." She sighed heavily, and for a while neither of them spoke as the car trundled down ever darkening narrow lanes. It felt intimate, the falling night, the lack of street lights, the heavy silence in the car, and yet somehow not uncomfortable.

Peter wondered if he should put the radio on. He was just reaching towards it when Samantha spoke.

"I would prefer not to work in close proximity to Dennis anymore, if that is at all possible."

Peter exhaled loudly.

"I knew it! What has he done?"

"Nothing, nothing!" She said too quickly. "He just makes me feel…uncomfortable is all."

A heartbeat of silence. The air in the car was too warm suddenly, the tension so thick it could be cut with a knife.

"You can tell me you know!" Peter's voice was almost pleading, almost wheedling. Of course, he knew already that something had happened when she had pretended to stub her toe.

Samantha didn't say anything, just turned her head and peered into the darkness. A few minutes passed by and then:

"We're nearly here, you can turn right after that house on the corner."

Some rectangles of orange lights appeared, lights in windows scattered in the murky landscape like windows of an advent calendar.

"You can let me out here."

Peter stopped the car in front of a nondescript row of three identical concrete houses. Utilitarian and unattractive. The middle one was blazing with light though.

"My flat mate is home already, that's good. I'll see you tomorrow!" Samantha leapt out too quickly as if escaping from Peter's questions. He stayed to watch the front door swing open and the orange light absorb her.

32

Despite the awkward atmosphere in the house, Poppy stuck to her guns and went out with Maisie. She was determined not to let anyone bully her, not even her perceived 'bestie,' Linda. University was supposed to be sociable and fun and Poppy wanted to go out and meet a variety of people, not be stuck with just one person who bossed her around. Poppy was still shocked by Linda's behaviour; she almost couldn't believe it. She had seemed so fun, so laidback, so friendly to everyone when they went out. How had Poppy misjudged her character so completely?

The night in the pub with Maisie and her new friends had been pleasant enough, although they had been shy, quiet people, and sometimes it had felt like an effort. However, coming home in the dark alone back to the silent bedsit had been creepy, even scary. At certain points, the roads around her abode were poorly lit and completely isolated and Poppy had not realised that, or at least not realised it fully, until that moment because hitherto, she had always been with Linda and not alone. She walked quickly and purposefully, her fingers grasped tightly around her keys so that they emerged from her small fist like metal claws.

Opposite the house, she couldn't bear to think of it as 'her' house, the pub was officially shut but there was clearly some sort of lock-in going on, slurred rough drunken voices carried on the wind and fragments of light shone behind tatty dark curtains.

Inside the house, there was complete darkness and silence. Poppy felt her spirits sink within her. She would have loved to chat to someone then, to talk about her evening, to gossip in the normal way, but since their argument, Linda had completely avoided her and Jason always kept himself to himself anyway. Only sometimes did he emerge from his lair and chat.

Poppy knew that she could have hardly expected that to change, for Jason to become more sociable, just because she was no longer getting on with Linda. In her tiny room, she propped the window open, and lit a cigarette into the wind. It used to be an intermittent habit, smoking, which she had recently adopted more enthusiastically. She kept her light off and let the street lights cast their maudlin shadows into her room. She sighed deeply as she exhaled. Rather than depressed, she was frustrated that she was stuck there in that house and annoyed with herself for misjudging Linda.

Several nights later, she went out with Tina's friends, and that, very unexpectedly turned into a more raucous affair. Poppy had not expected much from the evening as Tina had seemed so withdrawn and somehow sad when she and Linda had bumped into her, and yet the night was great fun. Tina had clearly put on her happy face. Whether it was sincere of not, there was no way of knowing.

They started with drinks in a packed pub but then went on to a student night at a club and stayed there, drunk and dancing until the early hours. Tina's friends were almost all her roommates from her halls, and they seemed to be mostly drama students, so they were extrovert and chatty and a bit manic. Tina seemed to have adapted her personality to fit theirs. The Tina who went out that night, and on subsequent nights, was a far cry from the subdued version that Poppy and Linda had encountered in the park that day; she seemed like a completely different person.

At the end of the night, in the freezing half-light of dawn, Tina asked Poppy whether she wanted to crash in their halls, and Poppy was hugely relieved that she did not have to make the miserable lonely journey back to her bedsit again.

There were four of them who made their way back to Tina's halls, exhausted and drunkenly linking arms; two boys, actors both, gay probably, Poppy and Tina. Poppy wondered if they were her new friends then, she hoped they were. She very much wanted to be adopted by fun people. Despite the ridiculous hour, most of the lights in the halls of residence they lived in, (an unattractive, rectangular building that resembled an office block from the outside), were shining brightly and a cacophony of various songs could be heard and drunk young voices laughing. The kitchen that they headed to and lounged about in was filthy more than merely grubby, and yet somehow Poppy didn't mind. One of the boys made them cups of tea and she didn't even think about whether the mug was clean, it didn't matter.

She spent that night in Tina's narrow bed. It was fortunate that both Poppy and Tina were quite small. It was uncomfortable but sticky warm, and even in her dreams, Poppy somehow knew there was no space to move and stayed still, in one position all night.

33

In the following weeks, at the Tensit high school, things did not improve for Simon, nor for Miss Sanchez. Both were clearly perceived as and treated as outcasts.

After that initial brief flurry of helpfulness (more than friendliness), Emily ignored Simon completely on the bus and in the school and at the bus stop. Whenever she saw him, in fact. Everyone ignored Simon except for Gary and his friends who would sometimes poke him in the side or jab at him or try to push him over for no reason at all. It was miserable for Simon. The only small consolation was that they were not in the 'A' group with him for most of their lessons.

The 'A' group, as suspected, contained the more diligent, academic students, mostly the girls. They were better behaved than the others certainly, but the academic standard was much lower than it had been in Simon's previous school in London. As time passed, he realised however, that this was not down to the teachers, as he had previously argued with his mum, but due to the total inertia and indifference of the students. The teachers tried hard to engage them but their attempts would be greeted with persistent blank stares. It was hard to watch, even for Simon, himself a teen of course, but a fair-minded sort of teen.

Because Simon made an effort to pay attention and respond to the teachers in class, he became, effectively, the 'teacher's pet' which emphasized his weird outsider status still further, and made things even harder for him.

"School is awful. It is horrible here." Simon was sitting at the kitchen table after school, his long limbs, as usual, sprawled awkwardly across the floor. "I don't know how much more of this I can take."

Bernice was fussing round him, offering tea and cake. She had found that excessive sugar helped a bit. The cupboards in the kitchen were now permanently stuffed with chocolate and sugary treats.

She listened to Simon complain every single day after school and was powerless to offer comfort. Bernice, herself, had helped Sarah a few more times to sweep the church and arrange flowers for a wedding (in a very basic way), but had so far resisted all entreaties to attend the church services or prayer meetings. Each time Bernice had helped was because she had happened to bump into Sarah in the village. It was never much fun, but she found, that once she was there, it was quite soothing to listen to Sarah's mundane chatter and was a mild balm for her own persistent loneliness.

Up until that point, she had not even bothered mentioning the Friday youth club run by Jacob to Simon, as she could have predicted exactly how that conversation would have gone. On that day, Bernice did, tentatively try to bring it up, not very successfully.

"I think," she began, "that we just need to alter the way that we perceive and judge the villagers."

"What do you mean?"

"We automatically hold them to the same standards as we used to apply to people in London, but that's a mistake, it will never work, as their development, their character development, I mean, has been completely different to that of city dwellers, of people who are brought up in cities, with the open-mindedness that inevitably entails."

"Even if that's true, I don't see how that theory helps us at all!"

"We have to lower our expectations, that's the gist of it."

"Hmm." Simon grunted.

"We could start by getting involved more…"

"You're kidding, right? I am absolutely as involved as I want to be by going to school, and that's only because it's a legal requirement!"

34

Peter told himself that he had no intention of trying it on with Samantha, of starting any kind of affair, and yet he found himself driving her home on a regular basis as Autumn progressed. The weather got colder and windier and Peter's heated car became a kind of cocoon. Music from an easy listening radio station played softly, and the darkness somehow emphasised the cosiness within. The two of them drove through those dusky isolated country roads as if they were navigating through their own private dreams.

It was unclear how the lift became routine, and yet within no time at all, Peter looked forward to the sight of Samantha standing next to his car, discretely at the end of the day, waiting for him patiently. He had taken to parking his car at the shadowy far end of the car park for the purposes of this discretion.

Meanwhile, Peter was trying really hard to relocate Dennis to London, but as he couldn't give a concrete reason for wanting to do so, those attempts were falling flat. The best he could manage was insisting to his boss that there was a terrible personality clash between the two of them, and having him moved to a different part of the factory.

As the factory was huge, this helped to a certain extent, but the administrative team itself was not that large, so inevitably Samantha still ran into Dennis now and again. Peter would know when she had seen him, even briefly, because she would appear downcast and miserable. This was notable because since Dennis had been relocated, Samantha had been a veritable ray of sunshine. Peter would reiterate his determination to try and expel Dennis entirely, but they both knew that he didn't have the authority and that the plan was futile.

Peter had been trying to console Samantha in the car on one particularly dark and blustery evening. It was the towards the tail end of October and Halloween was fast approaching. As usual the car was a cosy cocoon, a haven from the seemingly uncontrollable storm outside, and Peter's kind, albeit useless words were having their desired effect. Samantha relaxed completely and let her head slump on the headrest. She felt her eyes start to close and by the time Peter parked outside her house, she was snoozing lightly.

In the flattering half-light with the street lamp casting its lovely orange glow, Samantha seemed a fairy tale creature. Too beautiful for that town, or for Peter's car or, certainly, for Peter himself. He leant over, without thinking and kissed her deeply on her sleeping mouth.

That was the official start of it, probably. If one had to cite a time and a place. It could be argued that the affair had begun months previously when Peter had watched her carry coffee into a conference room, or a bit later when he had first offered her a lift. However, after the kiss it was officially an affair, there was no more potentially misunderstood innocence about it, it was exactly what it looked like. Samantha had opened her eyes wide and pulled him in, her soft hands light on the back of his neck.

After the kiss, it could have been stopped. Innocence could have been clawed back somehow. Peter could have made excuses not to drive Samantha, she could have made her weary way to the bus stop after work again. But he didn't and she didn't.

Samantha brought him into her house on that evening and on countless other evenings. Peter felt sheepish greeting her housemate, but not sheepish enough to stop what he was doing, what he intended to do.

Hours later, when Peter returned home, Bernice would have, dutifully, kept his dinner in the oven and he would recount elaborate lies about problems at the factory. His face would be flushed and his shirt often untucked and his hair would not look as if he had just walked in from an office.

35

In no time at all, Poppy, Tina and her two gay friends became a foursome who went everywhere together. They were huge partiers. They started in pubs and then went on to clubs, student nights in the main, bouncing to one after the other until the early hours, flitting about from one social group to another. They drank but they also took pills, mainly ecstasy, and speed, neither of which Poppy had done before and she was wary of both.

Poppy was puzzled at the change in Tina's personality, but she had never known her that well in London, so she told herself that Tina must have been having an off day when she had bumped into Poppy and Linda and been all withdrawn on that distant day in the park, because now, consistently, she seemed like an entirely different person. Perhaps the boys had brought something out in her, the party animal tendency which was hitherto lying dormant. The boys themselves were night creatures, they were not people who would ever partake in wholesome outdoor activities during the day. Poppy only ever saw them in the evening when they were all glammed up and hyped up and ready to go out.

Tina, on the other hand, she would also meet on campus for afternoon coffees, frequently. The girls, Poppy in particular, would joke that the boys were like vampires. They were studying geography and business respectively, and had very few in-person lectures to attend. Ergo, they spent most of the day asleep and lived for the evenings and the endless student nightlife.

"Still" commented Poppy soberly to Tina, "They won't get away with it for long, doing no work I mean."

"The first year is pretty unimportant." Tina shrugged. "Everyone says that."

Poppy must have raised her eyebrows because she continued then.

"I, personally, realised that I took everything too seriously in school. This is our opportunity to enjoy ourselves, probably our only real opportunity. It'll be far too late when we're old!"

Poppy nodded slowly.

"I get that, I do, but there is a fine balance. We don't want to be kicked out for not doing any work either, and there's always that possibility. Also, we won't be old for ages, we've got years ahead of us!"

Tina scoffed. Her face in the harsh daylight looked pinched and pale then.

"We don't know how long we've got, that's the problem." She commented, her tone much more serious suddenly, her mouth downcast. Tina had not shared with Poppy, yet, the reason that she had arrived late to Uni, Poppy wondered then, not for the first time, if someone close to her had died.

"Don't you like them, the boys I mean?" Tina asked suddenly.

They had got in the habit, early on, of referring to Tina's flatmates in her halls as 'the boys,' to the point that their real names were rarely, if ever, used.

"Gosh, yes, I like them a lot! I just think that they should study a bit more, for their own good I mean, that's all."

"You're not their mother, don't worry about it." Tina responded with unusual curtness.

Poppy looked at her sharply, surprised at her tone.

"What's happening with your housemate, anyway?" Tina's tone switched back to conversational. "Are you still not talking?"

Poppy sighed deeply.

"No, we're still not talking. It's really awkward actually. The house is horrible. The only positive thing about it was having someone there who I thought I got on with and now she is being super weird. It's a bit of a catch 22 actually, the more I go out, the more annoyed she is, I can tell by her face, whenever she walks past me…"

"A face like a slapped arse!"

"Exactly that, yes. But, on the other hand, there's no point staying there and sitting in my crappy little room on my own listening to them slaughter karaoke behind me in that awful pub."

"What about the other one, Jason is it?"

"Oh, he's super shy, he's not reliably there, if you know what I mean. Like sometimes, he'll be up for a chat, and sometimes, it's clear from the expression on his face that he doesn't want to talk."

36

"We don't celebrate Halloween in the village." Sarah announced to Bernice next time they met by accident. It was outside the shop where they usually ran into each other.

"Why ever not?" Halloween was not for adults in Bernice's opinion, but she was eager for any event to look forward to, and it had always been a huge deal in the suburb of London where they used to live. Bernice thought with a pang then of all the elaborate pumpkin-based decorations that had abounded everywhere. They would be displayed this year too, of course, only the Jensons would not be there to enjoy them.

"Well, it goes against the teachings of our church, of course." Sarah had become increasingly confident in her dealings with Bernice and her tone was sanctimonious and sharp.

Bernice sighed, "Yup, of course." She said dully.

"We do have the Harvest Festival though. That lasts all day, and it's great fun! There's a mass in the morning and then in the afternoon there is a barbecue and a party in a nearby field, weather permitting. If it's raining, we move to the church. Everyone brings food. It's usually very jolly."

Bernice had a hard time imagining that congregation as jolly. A thought came to her then.

"Are the whole village part of your congregation?"

Sarah narrowed her eyes at Bernice.

"What on earth do you mean by that?"

"Well…" Bernice faltered. She did not know why this woman now seemingly had the power to make her anxious.

"I just mean that, well, are there people who maybe don't go to your church, or go to a different church?"

"Different church?" Sarah sounded incredulous and stared at Bernice suspiciously, her eyes flinty in the harsh daylight.

"Why on earth would anyone travel to a different church when we have a perfectly decent one right here?"

"No reason," Faltered Bernice, "I just meant…"

"And the only villagers who don't come to church on a Sunday are your family now!" She remarked stiffly, her tone had gone belligerent almost and Bernice wished that she had kept quiet.

"Oh, I thought…" Bernice started feebly.

"The weekday mass and the prayer sessions are less popular that is true." Consented Sarah, "It's because of the additional cost…"

"Cost?" Bernice was genuinely baffled.

"Oh, don't worry about that yet!" Countered Sarah smoothly.

They were both standing on the pavement outside the shop. There was no one else around, a light drizzle had just started falling and the sky was an insipid shade of grey. Bernice hopped from foot to foot trying to think of an excuse which meant that she had to leave right away. She couldn't think of one. She couldn't claim she was off on a walk in this weather. Sarah, seemingly immune from the awkwardness, just stood there staring at her. The silence was unbearable.

"Harvest Festival sounds good!" Offered Bernice feebly, "We'll be sure to come to that!"

"You should come more often, you know, during the week too." Sarah was changing tack again apparently, her tone had grown smoother, more cajoling.

"It will help you meet people and form friendships you know. I know you are lonely here, who wouldn't be? Your husband and son away all day, and your son is older too, it's not as if he's a kid and you have to do every little thing for him."

"That's true." Bernice was relieved that Sarah was being nicer again. "When I had a job, I felt…"

"Pft!" Sarah sniffed. "Women do not need a job, they need to help their husbands and support their families and the way that you can do that is being cheerful and making friends in the village!"

"When you put it like that…" Bernice chose to ignore the bit about women not needing jobs. In a strange way, Sarah was starting to intimidate her. And that comment about 'cost' had thrown Bernice completely. It seemed bizarre given how shy and downtrodden Sarah had initially seemed and yet somehow it was true.

37

"A harvest festival? OK, why not?" Peter wasn't actually listening. They were in the living room, all three of them slouched on the old, yet supremely uncomfortable armchairs and sofa that had been left there. Sometimes they sat there instead of in the kitchen. It was a tough call as to which room was less cosy.

"Why isn't anything in this house comfortable?" Complained Peter. At least one such complaint was made by each member of the family on a daily basis. He was thinking about how much he missed Samantha. She had told him that she was busy that night, but had not elaborated. Unusually, she had left the office without saying goodbye. He didn't like that, it made him cross and twitchy and irrationally paranoid. He was staring unseeing at the television where a soap opera was playing, his mind ticking over relentlessly.

Simon was listening.

"What the actual fuck!" He exclaimed. "It is bad enough I have to see those people all day, now I have to see them on a Sunday too, give me a break!"

"Simon, language!" Said Peter automatically, without feeling.

Bernice sighed heavily again. Sometimes she felt that she spent all day every day sighing heavily. She had just got off the phone to Poppy and had been disappointed to hear that Poppy was not coming to visit them during her university reading week.

"Simon says it's all a bit grim there, he hasn't really been selling it to me." She told her mother. "Anyway, there are loads of Halloween parties on that week, it's a big thing in Nottingham, huge actually."

"Lucky you." Said Bernice, struggling to keep the bitterness and jealousy out of her tone, realising that it was absurd to be envious of your daughter's social life.

"There is absolutely nothing going on here. Enjoy yourself while you can."

Poppy was surprised to hear her mother so downcast and sounding so defeated.

"There must be an opportunity for you to make friends or maybe find a little job?" She suggested.

"Not in the village, it's far too small. Also, there's this church, Simon has probably already mentioned them. They're not very friendly, and they kind of dominate everything."

"What about further afield? Could you not maybe find something to do in that Tensit place where Simon goes to school?"

Bernice thought of the village bus and shuddered.

"Your father takes the car to work and the bus would be long."

Simon, overhearing Bernice's side of the conversation, rolled his eyes. The bus rides, both there and back to school, were the most miserable parts of his day. In that confined space, it was easy for Gary and his sycophants to push him about and poke him with their sharp fingers. His skin was riddled with bruises which he was careful to conceal under his clothes. It was much easier now that the weather had turned and freezing conditions were common. The village was completely exposed to harsh winds. Everyone wore thick shirts and woollen sweaters and jackets over their uniforms.

"Well, think about it at least." Poppy persisted, "It would be better than nothing, wouldn't it? Just a few days a week, maybe?"

"Hmmm." Bernice tried not to sigh again.

"When will we see you next then?"

"Christmas holidays probably."

"Oh. That's a long way away." Commented Bernice sadly.

"Why don't you come and visit me? Just for a day or so?"

"It's very far dear. I don't know. Let me think about it, I'll talk to your father and let you know."

"That's an excellent idea!" Peter had exclaimed immediately, when Bernice had told him about the invitation. He pictured lengthy evenings with Samantha for himself, without having to hurry home to his miserable wife.

Bernice stared at him in astonishment.

"It would be complicated and expensive, involving multiple trains!"

"I know that, dear, but I don't like to see you so miserable and the change of scene might do you good!"

Several things would happen then, in succession, and something else would appear to distract Bernice from her boredom, but neither of them knew that yet.

38

During breaks at school, Simon would habitually cower in a shadowy, isolated part of the school grounds. He would sit or crouch on the damp concrete on the border between the playground and the field which belonged to the school, and throw pebbles despondently at an ancient oak tree nearby. The enormous trunk hid him from anyone who happened to be watching him from the school building.

Simon often wondered how much misery this old oak had witnessed, how many lonely outcasts, just like him, had spent their breaks trying to be invisible behind its ancient trunk. There was something comforting about the pungent aroma of rotting vegetation under that tree, and Simon came to associate it with the brief flutter of relief that he felt there at breaktimes.

Of course, his tormentors knew that he was there, Simon could not kid himself otherwise. However, for some inexplicable reason, they usually left him alone during the breaks. Sure, there were enough other opportunities to get to him, the teachers nearly always turned a blind eye. They were basically free to bully him in class. Only Miss Sanchez would shout at them and try to get them to leave Simon alone. They always ignored her though. Simon had worked out that it wasn't because she was a woman, there were other female teachers that they listened to, that they seemed to respect; it was because she was Spanish. They didn't like outsiders in general, he himself could attest to that, and they definitely did not like foreigners.

It had turned much colder of late but still, Simon put on a thick jumper and a jacket over his grim uniform and went to crouch under what he began to consider as 'his' tree. Most of the other kids didn't even go out during the breaks when it was cold, they huddled in little groups in the dining room which always stank unpleasantly of cabbage and wet dish cloths. The boys would wrestle and kick a ball about until the dinner ladies yelled at them to stop.

Simon was unpleasantly surprised therefore to discern the sound of footsteps approaching him as he hid behind his tree one lunchbreak just before the October half term holiday. He had found a thick log to sit on that day. It was damp and probably teeming with insects but it was marginally more comfortable than the ground.

Simon looked up to find Emily manoeuvring herself behind the tree looking composed and pretty, as she usually did. He was relieved it was not one of his bullies, but he was still suspicious. Since that very first day when Emily had accompanied him to the classroom, she had ignored him. She had never participated in the bullying against him or the overtly bad behaviour towards Miss Sanchez, but neither had she ever helped either of them. He did not feel that he had to be particularly kind or polite to her, therefore.

"What do you want?" He asked, quite roughly, resenting the fact that he still fancied her, despite everything. Her hair, unusually, was not tied back in a bun that day and framed her pretty face perfectly, like a thick curtain.

"I want to apologise because I haven't been very welcoming."

Her cheeks glowed pinkly then, either from the cold or from embarrassment. It made her look even more becoming.

"It's a bit late now!" Huffed Simon, "It's been literally weeks and weeks, and honestly, I could certainly have done with a friendly face before now!"

"I know, I know, and I am sorry. It's just that…well, you've seen what they're all like! I grew up with them, they're all pretty awful as you can tell and I guess I…well, I guess I'm just too much of a coward to stand up to them. I…I don't want them to turn on me too."

"Why now though? Why would you come and say this to me now?"

"I felt bad. I mean, I have been feeling bad for ages and I have wanted to tell you for ages…"

"So, now that you know they are all inside and can't see you come and talk to me, now you gather the courage to…"

"Well, yes, I suppose so."

Emily nodded miserably. She had lowered herself down onto the same log that Simon was sitting on and stared quizzically at the great oak tree.

"Wow! That tree is kind of spectacular. I have never noticed it before."

"No, you wouldn't have." Said Simon quietly. "You would never have had a reason to come here."

39

It was a few days before Simon broke up for half term and the Harvest festival had yet to take place. Bernice had not 'bumped into' Sarah since the last intense chat they had had outside the shop, and she was nervous of bumping into her again. She had, therefore, spent even more time hibernating in the claustrophobic cottage.

At least the weather was conducive to hibernation. The winds were vicious that October and the area was often prone to the sort of horizontal rain which attacked you from the side leaving you completely drenched in seconds.

The only thing that had suddenly changed for the better was Simon's mood. Bernice was relieved to note that he seemed much perkier and less miserable than he had done since they had moved to Constance. Bernice had no idea what had induced such a change and Simon did not seem inclined to tell her. Still, for any mother, a child's happiness provides a boost.

It was a normal day, around mid-morning when the phone rang. Bernice, still in her dressing gown, had been telling herself that as the skies shone a rare bright blue and no doubt it would quickly cloud over, she should really get some fresh air and go for a walk. It would do her good, she was thinking, but at the same time, she really didn't feel like running into Sarah.

The man's voice was immediately familiar and she felt her breath catch in her own throat so that her own voice emerged squeaky and unnatural.

"Alex?" She squeaked.

"Aha! I've found you!" He sounded both jolly and matter of fact, and Bernice had to quickly remind herself that it had been months since she had last spoken to him, and that he had heavily implied that it was over between them the last time they spoke. Bernice took a deep breath and pulled herself together,

"I haven't been hiding," She told him, "I've been here all along."

"Yes, I know, I know, I've missed you, that's all."

Silence crackled down the phone line. Why was he being so friendly suddenly? What did he want?

"I've come to see you!" He exclaimed then, as if answering an unspoken question.

"What do you mean?" Bernice felt the prickling sensation of cold sweat as it settled on her skin.

"Where are you?"

"I'm in a hotel, if you can call it that, in the nearest town to you…Caver…"

"Cavershall?"

"Yes, that. Please come to meet me! I'll be here today and tomorrow. I took time out of my schedule to see you. This place is extremely grim, it would be much improved if you were here!"

"I never asked you to do that." Bernice responded dully, but her heart, nevertheless, was banging hard against her ribs in a kind of panicked excitement. She wasn't deluded enough to think that his intentions were pure but Alex would be a respite from her boredom and misery, she knew, that was certain and meeting him was very tempting.

"Surprisingly, I've spotted a lovely café here," he was using his most charming and cajoling tone, "It's not as magical as our café in London, but not bad, I think."

'Our' café. Inwardly Bernice snorted. He was a manipulative bastard and she knew it but she did want to see him, that was the sad fact of it.

"I don't have the car today, but I'll make up some excuse and get it tomorrow." She told him.

40

In the build up to Halloween, Poppy's social life became even more manic than it already was. She had taken to spending all her time, when she wasn't actually at lectures, at Tina's halls of residence and slept there often. Sometimes she shared Tina's bed or sometimes she crashed on a mattress that one of the boys had in his room.

Often, she wandered aloud what the mattress was doing there, but no one seemed to know. In any case they dressed it in a sheet and blankets and used it as an ad hoc guest bed. Poppy would often come to, her nose inches away from the dusty filthy floor, squinting at the detritus; abandoned socks and trousers and cigarette packets and boxes of condoms. It was all quite gross but she couldn't exactly say anything as the boys and Tina were so hospitable and friendly and never once insisted that she should go back home. They would have been well within their rights, after all. Their rooms were very cramped and they paid for them and Poppy, though tiny, still took up space.

It quickly got to the point where she only returned to the bedsit above the locksmith's shop to get changes of clothes or pick up work or books that she might have left there. She did all her college work at the library anyway. There was no space in her room. Sometimes she would shower there, but as she didn't want to bump into Linda, she often found herself queuing for the manky shower along with the other students in the halls of residence.

Halloween fell on an evening during 'Reading Week,' so it was the usual partying but on steroids as no one had to go to lectures. Poppy did have essays to write, but she struggled to find any motivation when she was always exhausted and hungover. Everyone said the first year didn't really count; that's what she told herself anyway.

Halfway through Reading Week, Poppy nipped back to the bedsit to pick up some more clothes. She was feeling particularly knackered, having had only a few disturbed hours of sleep on the mattress on the floor as the boys and some other kids carried on drinking and smoking in the room. Tina was not feeling well and had locked her own door so that she would not be disturbed.

They had been to a Halloween party in a club the night before. All of them had dressed as cats and painted their faces with black eyeliner and attached tails to their bottoms. On the following day, Poppy still had the remnants of whiskers around her nose when she went back to the bedsit.

She bumped into Linda on the stairs. In her hungover, but cheerful, haze, Poppy somehow imagined that Linda might be amenable to a friendly chat. That was not the case, however, far from it. Linda smirked as she walked down the stairs towards Poppy. In no way could it be misinterpreted as anything other than the sneer that it was. Poppy felt taken aback, although by then it shouldn't have surprised her. It still seemed like such an overreaction on Linda's part, though, to be so offended just because Poppy had other friends.

"Don't you ever wash your face? You'll get spots, you know."

Poppy smiled awkwardly.

"Eyeliner is quite hard to get off." She mumbled sheepishly. She felt awkward and self-conscious. The hallway smelt damp and foul. Tina's halls were filthy but at least they were not damp and did not possess this rank, pervasive stench.

"Your parents must be annoyed that they're paying for a room that you never stay in." Linda had stopped on the stairs and was leaning against the banister glaring at Poppy. She seemed to want a reaction, a fight, something.

Poppy didn't say anything. She didn't know what to say. Her parents didn't pay for anything; Poppy got a full grant. She was almost certain that Linda already knew that, that she, Poppy had shared that fact during the brief period that they had been friends. It was very common, during that era, to get a full grant.

Poppy lowered her gaze and made to edge past Linda on the stairs. There was enough space, the stairs were quite wide. She was shocked to feel a hand shove against her shoulder, aggressively enough that it would later leave a bruise. Poppy stumbled onto the lower step but did not fall. She stared for one second straight into Linda's face, both horrified and hurt.

41

Simon still fancied Emily, even more so now that she was officially his friend.

Not that she ever went out of her way to advertise that fact. On the bus to school, for instance, she still sat next to her sister and Simon was left to fend for himself, just as he had always done. In lessons too, she did speak to him, but not much, certainly not enough to negate the mountains of antagonism stacked against him on a daily basis from Gary and his gang of fools. It was more that she acknowledged him during classes, whereas previously she had ignored him completely.

It was during the breaks that she was most present, physically next to him under the oak tree. It wasn't that brave of her, he had to admit that to himself. In the freezing cold and bitter wind, nobody else braved the outdoors and therefore no one else bore witness to their friendship.

As long as it wasn't actually raining, the two of them piled on layer upon layer and sat chatting under the tree during mid-morning break and after they had both eaten their lunch, (Simon alone and Emily with her friends, as usual.)

Simon found Emily's character to be interesting but complex. On the one hand, she was more naïve and innocent in many ways compared to the girls he had known in London, those street-wise, trendy city kids, accustomed to navigating the humdrum unpredictable streets of the metropolis. Yet, on the other hand she was harder in many ways, there was the same cold cruelty about her, although slightly less of it, that he saw in the rest of his classmates and in the faces of the congregation at the church in Constance. She had a high degree of intolerance towards foreigners of all kinds, especially people of other races. Neither did she believe that women needed to be educated beyond high school.

Simon had discovered that strange fact when he had asked her what she wanted to be, what job she might like to have. He, himself, had always been fascinated by law and could picture himself arguing in a courtroom.

"That's a fancy ambition!" She had sniffed somewhat scornfully. "It's not fancy, it's normal." Simon had felt genuinely puzzled. In London it had been normal.

"Why? What would you like to do?"

"Well, get married, of course and have kids."

"No, I mean as a job?"

"I don't really want a job, if at all possible, I would just like to stay at home." She shrugged.

"Yes, but…" Simon was genuinely baffled. "Don't you want to do anything? I mean, even if it's impractical, like acting or dancing or writing?"

"Writing? Are you kidding? That's way too hard! You'll find most kids round here aren't academic like you, they just want some menial job to get by. I suppose a lot of girls end up being beauticians or working in shops in Cavershall if they have to but, personally, I don't see the appeal myself."

"But…" Simon was confused. "You are smart! You're in class with me remember? Lots of people in that group are really smart, why don't they want to do anything more with their lives?"

"I guess because we have never left this area. We don't know anything 'more' as you put it, and we don't want anything more." She shrugged. "Obviously, you see things differently because you come from the big bad city!"

"It's really not that bad." Simon laughed.

"Yeah right!" Emily smirked, looking sceptical.

"No, it really isn't! It's busy, yes, and fast-moving, and the traffic is usually terrible, but it's absolutely fine apart from that."

"That's not what they tell us, you know." Said Emily.

42

Bernice was expecting more scrutiny from Peter when she asked to use the car the following day, but surprisingly he had just nodded vaguely. She mumbled something about having to find a dentist, but his eyes were glazed over and she could tell he wasn't listening.

It was early evening in the kitchen and Peter had returned from work much earlier than he had been doing of late. In fact, it had been several days in a row that he had returned early.

"Things must be going well," Bernice had commented cheerfully, "I see they're letting you out earlier these days!"

Peter, already sitting at the table staring at a newspaper had glanced up at her with a strangely blank expression. Bernice had been a bit taken aback.

"What's wrong? You don't seem yourself?"

"I'm fine." He scowled, clearly irritated by the question, "Just tired, is all."

Bernice busied herself at the counter so that he could not see the grin on her face. Despite everything, despite knowing that nothing good would come of it, she was excited to see Alex the next day. Whether it was him that she missed or whether it was just that her life in Constance was so boring and miserable that she was longing for any distraction, that was a matter for debate.

It was a lovely sunny day and they had arranged to meet directly at the 'lovely' café that Alex had mentioned. Bernice doubted that it was, in fact, 'lovely.' She could not imagine any establishment in the cold, soulless landscape of Cavershall fitting that description, and yet, having looked it up on a map, Bernice realised that it was located down a lane she had not realised was there. How would she have realised? She had only been there the once in order to get Simon's uniform, and on that occasion, they have only really seen the grim high street and the department store.

In any case, she was pleasantly surprised to note that there was a prettier, albeit very contained, part of Cavershall, hidden away behind its miserable façade. It consisted of a few, short, pedestrianised lanes full of quirky gift shops, cafes, and boutiques. Unlike the dull office blocks situated on the main streets, the brightly-painted buildings there were old-fashioned low-ceilinged cottages, prettily decorated and festooned with late- blooming flowers in red planters.

Bernice was still reeling from the shock of this discovery when she walked into the café where she had arranged to meet Alex. The fashionable, arty café located in such a grim town seemed like an omen of sorts, she wasn't sure of what.

Bernice's gaze swept nervously over the assorted clientele before settling on the middle-aged man sitting at the window. She recognised Alex by his jacket. Although she must have passed him to enter the café, he did not turn his head to look at her, and in that instant, she realised that this was already a power trip for him and by giving in and coming to meet him, she was making a mistake.

Still, the alternative would be to walk out then, and with all her heart, she did not feel like doing that. Instead, she arranged her expression into a smiley one and when he turned his head, she was pleased to note that he was smiling too. His skin, however, looked more ravaged than she had previously noticed as if the process of ageing had somehow accelerated on him in the intervening months.

"You're a sight for sore eyes." Alex told Bernice and his voice reeled her in and took her back via a spinning series of images, through a history of their affair. The friendliness and then the loneliness, the casual cruelty and manipulation and then the friendliness again. She had understood it at the time and she understood it now and yet here she was, once again, sitting before him, the bright sunlight pouring through the window and straight onto her hopeful face.

43

Samantha was avoiding Peter and he didn't know why. It was making him miserable. It had been nearly a week, by then, not only of Samantha taking the bus home, but also of her refusing to talk to him beyond the most cursory work-related chat. He had tried asking her directly whether something was wrong and she had told him that no, there wasn't. Her body language, however, told a different story; she completely avoided eye contact or standing anywhere near him or even brushing against him by accident.

Obviously, there was something wrong but there was no way that matters could be clarified if Samantha refused to talk to him or let him drive her home, even if only to chat.

Peter even wished he had someone to confide in about this strange scenario, but of course he did not. He racked his brains to try and pinpoint something he had done, something offensive. He couldn't think of anything beyond the obvious cheating situation, and surely that had been transparently clear to Samantha right from the start?

Peter really struggled to concentrate at work. Things had progressed well in the factory since the right machines had been delivered, so there weren't any imminent catastrophes, but he was painfully aware that he should have been keeping his eye on the ball, and he wasn't.

Dennis was now officially employed at the other end of the factory, and yet, much to Peter's (and no doubt, Samantha's) dismay he could often be seen lurking in the corridor outside Peter's office. It was disconcerting, to say the least. Also, a bit creepy. Maybe it was that which was bothering Samantha? But if that was the case, there was no reason for her not to confide in Peter. Dennis was the enemy of them both; that was how Peter saw it, and that had seemed clear from the start of their affair.

To add to the confusion, Samantha had taken to dressing differently of late. Peter could not put an exact date on when he had noticed the change. To him, she had seized to be just a sexy body within weeks and had become something more. He realised, within days of them lying together in Samantha's small double bed in her girlish room with the cheap pine furniture, that he had been desperate for the connection that he had long since lost with his wife. Not just the physical connection, but also the companionship.

Peter didn't notice immediately, therefore, that Samantha had stopped dressing in a sexy manner. It was more of a sudden realisation, one afternoon, when he had looked up at her approach with a file that he had asked for and he noticed that she was wearing the sort of long, shapeless burgundy dress that he would usually associate with someone elderly or overweight; someone who was trying to hide her body in any case, not reveal it.

As she had walked out of his office then, without a word, he had realised with a start that for days she had been wearing the same, or a very similar dress, and his bafflement deepened.

Bernice had been acting strange too. The excuse she had given, on the day she had borrowed the car, had obviously been a lie. He had known immediately that it was a lie, and that was only confirmed later that same evening when Peter had asked Bernice how the dentist had been and she had said "What?" and looked startled before quickly backtracking and mumbling some nonsense about an emergency filling. She had eaten her dinner completely normally though; she wasn't chewing on one side or acting as if one side of her mouth was delicate, as one would expect.

What was she up to? She seemed energised and happier and it certainly was nothing to do with the village. Simon had told them that they should 'try out' the harvest festival, on the basis that there was 'nothing else to do.'

That was true, of course, but Peter was very surprised that Simon suddenly wanted to go. He had shown absolutely zero interest in anything to do with the church up until that point.

44

It was breakfast time and the Sunday of the Harvest Festival was unusually bright and much warmer than anticipated. Bernice was glad, not for herself, but for Simon who seemed strangely enthusiastic about a social outing. Bernice had not witnessed that particular side of him, his usual youthful energy, since they had left London.

"They'll be a girl involved, you mark my words. That'll be the reason for this sudden change of heart." Commented Peter drily. He was sitting staring at the Sunday newspaper which was laid out before him on the kitchen table. Bernice had the uncanny impression though, that he was not reading it. She had no idea what had come over Peter recently. He looked pale and drawn, but whenever Bernice asked him if he was ill, he looked irritated and shook his head. The couple had had little to say to each other in recent years, that was true, but Peter's current silence seemed quite excessive and alarming.

Probably, Bernice didn't dwell on it as much as she should have done, as her head was, once again, full of Alex. In the quirky café in Cavershall, after a bit of stilted conversation, things had warmed up, and soon they were flirting with each other again. The atmosphere was warm and giggly, reminiscent to how they had been with each other at the very start of their affair. Alex acted the part of a caring and charming man, and kept reiterating how much he had missed Bernice and how he had realised that he couldn't actually live without her. His dog, under the table, had whined when she had sat down and buried its soft head in her lap.

Bernice had felt something within her melt and relax, but also, simultaneously, a quickening, a thrill jolt through her. She knew, deep down of course she knew, that he, Alex, was manipulating her all over again, for his own dark purposes, and yet, somewhat flippantly, she did not care.

In Constance, she was more bored than she had ever been in her life, and the alternatives which had been presented to her, namely helping out in the weird church, were unappealing to say the least. This, whatever this was, was certainly wrong, yes, but it was also exciting and fun, and Bernice really craved, really needed, some fun and excitement.

That day in the café in Cavershall with Alex had been innocent, in the physical sense, anyway. Bernice had driven home directly afterwards, so elated that even the treacherous narrow country roads hadn't managed to burst her bubble. However, Alex had told her he would be down again soon and regularly and they needed to arrange somewhere discrete to meet. Bernice knew he did not mean for a cup of tea, and her heart pounded in her chest so loudly that she could hear it.

Probably, had the rest of her life not been so dry, she would not have been so desperate to jump into bed again with Alex. That Sunday, for instance, Bernice had the whole Harvest Festival charade to get through and because she had something else to look forward to, she didn't even mind.

Simon came down to breakfast fully dressed in neat clothes with his hair brushed, an unheard-of phenomenon. Bernice raised her eyebrows and tried to catch Peter's eye, but he was still scowling miserably at the newspaper, and apparently had not even noticed his son.

The day before, Sarah had caught up with Bernice in the street, literally jogged up behind her as Bernice was striding along, deep in her daydreams, oblivious.

"I could really use some help with the decorations, all the flowers and so forth for the festival tomorrow…" She had stared at Bernice with a petulant expression, her voice slightly whiney.

Bernice was feeling stronger though, for better or for worse, her meeting with Alex had reminded her that she had had a life before Constance, she had a brain and could stand up for herself, in some aspects of her life anyway. She wasn't going to let Sarah manipulate her and make her feel guilty.

"Sorry no," She had said then, "I'm busy."

45

Bernice put on a plain, smartish navy dress and Peter, still in his weird, dissociative state, had to be persuaded to run a comb through his hair. His jeans and jumper looked crumpled and even a bit grubby. It was extremely unusual for him to be so neglectful and careless of his appearance, and even Bernice, distracted as she was, felt a twinge of panic. What if there was something seriously wrong with him? One heard all sorts of things. It could be physical, it could even be mental, she knew. Early onset dementia, some kind of nervous breakdown, all sorts of things! Even though she no longer loved him, Bernice certainly didn't want any harm to befall Peter. She determined then, as they walked into the packed church, to keep a better eye on him, even as she planned to embark on the second phase of her illicit affair.

Simon walked into the church smiling and obviously looking around for someone. Had Peter been his normal self, Bernice would have nudged him so they could both enjoy their son's happiness, but the way he was then, there was no point. Bernice tried to follow Simon's gaze but the hall was packed with everyone still standing and greeting each other, the normally dry people in more jovial spirits than usual.

The Jensons sat at the back with Simon next to the aisle, where he was still looking around frantically, like a meerkat. When everyone had quietened down and was seated and waiting for the service to commence, Bernice had a chance to appreciate the effort that had gone into decorating the uninspiring space for the harvest festival, no thanks to her, of course.

Bouquets of sunflowers and chrysanthemums were dotted about everywhere as well as little families of variously sized pumpkins. Bernice was impressed and wondered, in an abstract way, whether Sarah had managed to rope anyone in to help her. It stood to reason, within a congregation which did not believe that women should work, that there were many bored housewives itching to do anything to while away the time.

Notwithstanding the more jovial atmosphere, the service was just as long and boring as it had been before. Peter lowered his chin to his chest and appeared to nod off. He resembled, in that vulnerable position, a much older man, and Bernice felt, within her again, the uncomfortable weight of concern. Simon, meanwhile, was staring rapt at someone in front of him that Bernice could see only partially, when the tall person in front of her moved. It was certainly a girl though, there were two of them who looked virtually identical from the back, both had tight ballet-dancer buns and long slim necks. Content as she was to observe her much happier son and try and spy on the object of his interest, the dull drone of Robert's voice eventually did for Bernice too and by the time the lengthy service ended, she was half-asleep, pleasantly dozing and daydreaming of being elsewhere.

The plan, after the service, was to have a barbecue and a gathering in a nearby field which was located on the edge of the village and belonged to a local farmer. After the service, no one really acknowledged the Jensons, which was a bit depressing. One would have thought that during a supposed celebration, the congregation would try and be a bit more friendly, but apparently not. Maybe, thought Bernice, we are just not trying hard enough. Simon on leaving the church, looked a bit deflated, although his eyes were still glued to the girl or girls, who were walking with their parents someway in front of them.

As before, everyone had to walk past Robert, Sarah, and Jacob on exiting the church. Bernice couldn't help but notice that Sarah seemed to glower at her unpleasantly. Clearly, she had not been forgiven for refusing to help decorate the church. Bernice still felt defiant, but her confidence was tinged with a glimmer of unease. She could sense how powerful that family was.

46

On the morning after the last Halloween party, Poppy woke up in bed with Tina, with virtually no recollection of what had happened the night before. She had been shocked into wakefulness suddenly, by the sight of an abundant red smear of what appeared to be blood on Tina's sheets. It took a second for Poppy's hungover brain to recall that they had been playing around with a silly vial of fake blood in Tina's room the night before and, inevitably, it had splashed all over the bed.

Since Linda had pushed her on the stairs, Poppy had only rarely been back to the bedsit, and only when it was absolutely essential that she picked something up that she needed. Poppy and Tina had had numerous discussions about how she could transfer to the university halls of residence, but the bedsit had been paid for a term in advance, so she could not possibly move before January, and even then, it was by no means certain that there would be a vacancy in that hall or any of the others. There certainly hadn't been in September, which was why Poppy had ended up at the bedsit in the first place.

Poppy couldn't crash with Tina and the boys indefinitely, she knew that. The hall they were in was poorly managed and disorganised, certainly, but the night manager had taken to staring at Poppy and frowning whenever she scuttled up the stairs past him. It was only a matter of time before they worked out that she was not supposed to be there.

The idea of sleeping at the bedsit now, however, of even returning there, was scary for her; Poppy literally shuddered at the thought. With her aggressive gesture, Linda had switched from merely unfriendly to borderline psychotic and Poppy never wanted to see her again. She couldn't believe that she had briefly considered Linda to be a great friend, even a best friend.

Because she was young, and often drunk and emotional, all Poppy's feelings were quite extreme at that point. Was Linda legitimately dangerous? Probably not. However, in the alcoholic fuzz they all resided in semi-permanently, emotions were heightened and stories were recounted and exaggerated in order to entertain their audience, mainly each other; they tended to egg each other on.

At some point one of the boys asserted that he had seen Linda hanging out in front of the humanities building where Poppy had lectures, that Linda had been 'loitering with intent.'

"Oh!" The other boy exclaimed dramatically, covering his face with his thin hands, "Do you think she might be stalking Poppy now?"

And although Poppy had not believed in the possibility of Linda becoming an obsessed stalker, not at the time of the drunken conversation nor after, she, nevertheless found herself glancing over her shoulder whenever she was alone to make sure that she wasn't being followed. Whether it was subconscious or not, she wouldn't have been able to say, but it was just a thing that she did. When she returned to the bedsit, which was only in absolute dire necessity, she got one of her new best friends to come with her.

The boys would treat visits to the bedsit as if they were outings to a famous haunted house which was a bit trying. They would creep around the damp building as if they were acting on a stage or on a film set. Poppy found that it was better to take Tina, she was more discrete and far less given to unnecessary drama.

Since the day that Linda had pushed her, Poppy had not seen her but one day, when she had popped in with Tina to pick up more clothes, she did bump into Jason. He was emerging from the kitchen and when he saw Poppy a strange look had settled on his face. He looked annoyed, certainly unfriendly. Poppy didn't think he would stop to speak to her then, but he did.

"I'm sorry that you felt the need to move out."

He spoke as if he was personally offended by Poppy's absence, which she found a bit odd. She wasn't sure how to react.

"I haven't officially moved out." She said lamely, "That is why I have to keep returning to pick up my clothes."

"Still!" Snorted Jason huffily as he moved past her and shut the door to his room behind him.

"Still, what?" Asked Tina baffled.

"No idea." Said Poppy.

47

Simon had somehow thought that Emily would acknowledge him in church, or at least on the way in or out. He hadn't been expecting a big gesture; just a little wave would have sufficed. But there had been nothing and she had definitely seen him. Before the service had started, she had turned in her seat and stared right at him with her huge eyes and the curiously vacant expression that they all wore so well and so habitually, as if it was part of the doctrine of the church itself.

Along with his parents, Simon followed the crowd as they all headed to the designated field for the barbecue. The sun was high in the sky and it was unseasonably warm for that time of year. People kept their thick coats open and unfurled their woollen scarves from about their sweaty necks. The atmosphere was joyful and friendly, but not towards the Jensons. They seemed to manoeuvre down the road with an unbreachable forcefield around them; no one came close.

Simon held onto a sliver of hope that at the barbecue, Emily would be able to get away from her parents and become friendlier. She had been the one who persuaded him to come to the harvest festival, after all. She was the only reason he had come and dragged his poor parents along. Why had she told him to come if she just intended to ignore him?

His dad looked as if he should have been in bed instead. He seemed strangely pale and peaky. His mum looked happier than Simon had seen her in a while, but distracted, as if she was permanently thinking of something else.

A huge marquee had been erected in the field and various stalls had been set up within it. One could buy snacks of various kinds, pastries or cakes or drinks. Outside the marquee, an enormous barbeque area had been set up. It consisted of a very old-fashioned grilling contraption, which would have been more at home at an antique's fair. Two rotund men were manning it. Both wore aprons and one of them was brandishing a pair of massive tongs.

"I think that must the butcher from a nearby village," commented Bernice.

"That makes sense," Replied Simon.

Already a crowd was forming around the barbecue as if it was a spectator sport. In fact, apart from the consumption of food there was not much else to do. The much younger, less self-conscious kids had joined forces and run off together to the other end of the field, whereas the older, more awkward teens were still mooching around with their parents. The whole event had about it a stiff formality, no one seemed very relaxed, that was how Simon felt.

Vividly, he recalled then, similar events that had been held in his schools in London, how the kids had run riot and the parents had hung out together and got drunk. The whole atmosphere had just felt much more relaxed and fun than this.

"Don't you want to, I don't know, hang out with some young people?" Asked Bernice.

"Young people!" Simon scoffed, "Does it look as if any of these 'young people' want to hang out with me?"

In fact, apart from Emily, various of Simon's classmates were there, including his bullies. All of them were stuffed into their uncomfortable-looking Sunday best, and looked nearly as miserable as he felt.

"I don't think any of them want to hang out with us." Sighed Bernice. "I think I'll just get something to eat and then take your father home, I don't know what's wrong with him but he looks unwell."

Peter was standing on the fringes of the group contemplating the barbecue, but he himself seemed to be staring blankly into the distance instead.

"Good idea." Agreed Simon, "He looks weird."

"It'll warm up you know and get better." A familiar voice behind them suddenly piped up. Simon turned abruptly to see Emily standing there, alone. Bernice scuttled off tactfully to one side.

"Will it really?" Asked Simon, aware that his voice was thick with sarcasm, "Get better, I mean? How exactly? Alcohol would make it better, even if it was only for the adults, but I haven't seen any!"

"Good point and no, Robert doesn't believe in alcohol, not for his flock."

"His flock need cheering up though!" Said Simon.

"You're probably right." Emily chuckled. "Shall we go for a walk?"

Simon stared at her astonished. "What about your parents?"

"You want to go for a walk with my parents?" Emily laughed.

"Very funny, you know what I mean!"

"Oh, they don't mind. They know we go to school together. Anyway, we'll only be in the field where they can see us."

"Yeah, right, of course."

48

Peter had not been feeling well, that much was true. He looked how he felt which was pale, lethargic, and weak and somehow fragile, but without the fever which would indicate a bug of some kind. The onset of the malaise seemed to have coincided with Samantha's rejection, and initially, he had attributed the physical symptoms to a moderate depression, even though that seemed odd. Never before had he noticed any sadness translate into a physical illness. He didn't really believe that could happen.

It was probably also the stress of running the factory, Peter told himself. It truly did seem that no sooner had he resolved one problem, that another issue popped up to take its place, often more than one simultaneously.

That day, at the harvest festival, he felt spaced out more than anything. He wanted to be at home in the peace and quiet alone. Bernice had offered to take him home, but Peter, somewhat brusquely, had insisted that he would return home on his own. Bernice, well, most people really, got on his nerves. He didn't want anyone bustling around him, anyone near him, anyone asking him questions and fussing.

Bernice finally agreed, with a small worried smile, and told him that she would bring him some food back. He nodded indifferently and headed home with the strange exaggerated stoop of someone who was prematurely old.

Bernice would have preferred to have the excuse that she needed to accompany Peter home. She was hanging around at the barbecue like a spare part. Simon had gone off with Emily, about which she was pleased. At least one member of the family was not a complete outcast. She could see the two of them walking around the edges of the field. She loitered around on the fringes of the barbecue for want of anything else to do. The longer she was ignored, the more awkward she felt.

Bernice had just decided that she would buy some food, any food, to take back to Peter, when Sarah bustled up to her. Sarah was wearing a voluminous flowery flock which draped over her huge frame like an unflattering tent.

"You wouldn't be so lonely if you integrated more." She declared, smirking at Bernice.

"I am not lonely, thanks." Bernice replied through gritted teeth. "I am absolutely fine on my own because I am happy with my own company!" The flippancy emerged without effort and Bernice was happy to go with it.

"If you say so." Said Sarah, still wearing the weird smirk, but looking a bit shocked at the defiant reply.

"Oh, I do." Said Bernice, smirking back.

"You know that Robert has a lot of contacts at the factory."

Bernice paused, genuinely confused.

"What do you mean by that?"

"Nothing. I am just letting you know, as a kindness." With that, Sarah turned on her heels and walked away, the tent-like garment flapping behind her in the breeze.

Bernice stood still feeling her face burning. She sensed other people around her observe her and lean into their friends to gossip. More than anything, she felt confused and then angry. She no longer cared what these cold, boring people felt about her. What had brought about that change? Seeing Alex again? Maybe it was just that seeing him had reminded her of her life in London and the better people, the more open and friendly people that she had been surrounded by there.

They couldn't be stuck in that hideous village forever, surely? It clearly wasn't doing Peter any good and Simon obviously hated his school. Bernice glanced over to the field but Simon was nowhere to be seen. She turned her back on the lot of them and walked home without buying any food.

49

"Aren't you going to get into trouble?" Simon and Emily had climbed over a stile and moved past the original field into another one. Emily had led the way and Simon had followed, but still he was concerned that he would eventually be blamed for this transgression. Emily's parents looked quite severe, like the rest of the congregation, they appeared rigid and humourless, with pale pinched faces etched with some kind of chronic disapproval.

"We'll just say that we were in a group of friends from school, if they ask." Emily shrugged.

"They'll buy that?" Simon was thinking that no one would believe that he was hanging out with a group of friends from school.

"On these days, they tend to be a bit more relaxed. They'll have a drink eventually and, anyway, they tend to worry about my sister more as she's younger…"

"Hang on a second, a drink? I thought there was no alcohol at these things?"

"Not officially no, but many of the men have a little hip flask they bring with them in their inside pockets."

"Wow."

"You're from London, surely it's not that shocking!"

"It's the hypocrisy of it that's shocking, the dishonesty! Why not just say that drinking is allowed without the need for all the secrecy?"

Emily looked as if she was about to get annoyed but then just shrugged.

"I guess it's just the way it is around here." She said mildly. "Are you coming or not?" She grabbed his hand and her tiny fingers felt fragile and cool in his.

They walked silently through the field, full of sunflowers tilting their nodding heads at the sun still bright overhead, towards a dense wood on the far side. Simon wondered what the plan was, but didn't say anything. Barely any sunlight or warmth filtered through the trees in the wood and both kids shivered at the sudden lowering of temperature. It was instinctive for Simon to put his arm around Emily's slim shoulders and she let him. She was wearing a navy dress of some scratchy fabric, a woollen coat on top, smart and formal, like those worn by small children to a private prep school with their names sewn into the collar.

There was no path through the wood, the ground was uneven and littered with shrubs and fallen branches and unexpected pits of sunken earth. It was not a comfortable walk and Simon was relieved when they arrived at a tiny clearing and Emily sat down immediately on a conveniently-placed log. She seemed to know it was already there. Simon was sure in that instant that she had been there before. Something bothered him about that perceived fact, but he didn't have time to dwell on it at that moment because Emily started kissing him. She just turned towards him as they sat on the log and held his chin with her cold fingers and manoeuvred it towards her face.

Simon had kissed girls before and could tell that it was not the first time for Emily either. There was a confidence there which seemed at odds with her strict religious family, but later he would realise that there was a great deal of wilful pretending that went on in that community, more than he would ever have thought possible.

Both Simon and Emily were enjoying themselves so much, (and they had their arms around each other's heads so that their hearing was compromised), that they did not hear the sound of twigs snapping or the muffled gleeful exclamations of Gary and his cronies as they approached.

50

On Monday morning, Peter was relieved to realise that he felt much better suddenly. On waking, he stood up feeling revitalised and refreshed from a deep sleep and much like his old self. Bernice was happy to see him look perkier and told him so. They had a friendly, albeit superficial exchange, and Peter got into his car determined to put his best foot forward at work.

No sooner had he pulled into the car park of the factory, however, when a pall seemed to be cast over him, as insidious as a dense cloud. It was a seemingly unshakeable sense of gloom. At least I know now, he told himself, grappling to find a bright side; at least I know that it is this factory that is making me feel ill. Still trying to shake the malaise, he walked past Samantha to get to his office and was surprised that she greeted him with a warm smile.

"When you have a minute, Peter," She said, "I would like to have a chat. I think I owe you an explanation."

"Of course, of course, let me just look at my diary..."He fumbled.

"I have your diary, Peter," Said Samantha with a small tight laugh, "You are busy with meetings until late afternoon, shall we schedule our chat for 4pm? Does that suit you?"

Peter would have given anything to cancel his meetings and chat with Samantha then and there, but he had to at least seem as if he was taking his job seriously. He went about his day on auto-pilot, trying his best to focus on what was being said in meetings, but realised that his thoughts were drifting away, untethered. Dennis was in one of the meetings and Peter found himself watching him surreptitiously. The man always seemed to have a sly smirk on his face as if he was up to no good.

Peter wondered then, not for the first time, what Dennis had done to Samantha, or tried to do. He determined to ask her about it when they met at four, it was time to get everything out into the open.

At 3.45pm, Peter was in his office literally counting down the seconds by watching the ticking hand of the huge arty modern clock that some misguided decorator had attached to his wall. Exactly two minutes later a siren blared throughout the whole factory. It did not sound like a normal office fire alarm, for some reason it sounded like an air raid siren from the second world war, and Peter remained still in his chair for long seconds, frozen in shock.

Why now? He thought, anguished. Why now when he was about to talk to Samantha and finally clear the air? Had Dennis set it off? Peter's paranoid mind rumbled away searching for reasons and conspiracies where there weren't any. By the time he mobilised himself to leave the office and walk down the stairs to the car park where they were supposed to congregate, everyone else had already gone, the whole factory felt empty. Peter's footsteps echoed in the concrete stairwell and he wondered if he was the only one left in the burning building. He sniffed and told himself that he could smell smoke very distantly, but by then he was struggling to trust his own senses and he didn't know if he was imagining it or not.

As it turned out, there was a small fire on the factory floor. Part of one of the new machines had mysteriously burst into flames. All the machines were immediately shut down and everyone was evacuated, no harm done.

In the car park, Peter saw all of his colleagues milling around and chatting excitedly in clusters. For him, Peter thought wearily, this fire and the associated health and safety issue would just be the makings of a new headache. He couldn't see Dennis, nor Samantha though in the car park. When he asked, he was told that Samantha had left.

Peter had no reason, at the time, to believe that she was not coming back.

51

Gary smacked Simon around the head. Both Emily and Simon jerked their heads round to see him and his ferrety little gang surrounding them, still incongruously clad in their old-fashioned church-going attire. The half-light under the trees seemed suddenly not romantic but ominous.

Simon swallowed but found that his throat felt dry and prickly. Gary was looming over him. Seated as the couple were, Gary and his goons seemed massive.

An expression of glee was shining over Gary's malevolent pallid face. Simon was outnumbered and vulnerable here with no adults around to save him.

"You come over here," taunted Gary in a silly, mocking tone, "You steal our women!"

"I am not your woman, Gary, as you well know!" Emily, Simon was amazed to realise, was not even scared, or if she was, she certainly didn't sound it.

He dared to hope that maybe Gary's bark was worse than his bite. Unfortunately, however, that proved not to be the case.

"Get him!" Shouted Gary and the three other boys leapt on Simon, where he was still being held down by Gary on the log. They pummelled him with their fists and kicked him with their ridiculous church-going smart shoes. Simon knew that he could have taken any of them on, individually, in a fair fight, but this was not a fair fight and against all of them together he had no chance.

Unlike at school or on the bus, they appeared to believe that here in the isolated wood, they were in a lawless terrain and it did not matter how bruised Simon was. Even in the midst of it, as Emily was screaming, and Simon was curled up on the damp cold ground trying to protect his face, he wondered whether they believed that they were invincible, that no one would punish them for this violence inflicted on him.

Or was he, Simon, just irrelevant to the village as a whole? Somehow, less than human to the community?

Emily tried to leave to get help. Simon knew that Gary was holding her with one arm. He feared, even whilst suffering the agonising blows to his own tender flesh, that they would try to do something to Emily. They seemed, that day, to have no boundaries.

Simon passed out at one point, rendered unconscious, most likely, by a blow to the head. When he came too, minutes later, the pain hit him anew, they were still bashing him, and for the first time he let himself cry. He had the urge to call for his mother, but resisted. Emily was crying in great sobs and still screaming.

They stopped suddenly and for no apparent reason. Although later, Emily and Simon would speculate that they had stopped because they must have heard someone else in the wood. They stopped, conferred together in murmurs, let go of their captives and ran, stumbling awkwardly across the undergrowth.

Simon was lying in a foetal position on the ground and Emily was sitting next to him. She put her hand on him gently and then rested her head on his shoulder. Both of them were sobbing. They stayed there a long time until the adrenaline drained from them and the cold hit.

"We should take you to a doctor or a hospital" Emily whispered, her voice trembling.

"Absolutely not!" Mouthed Simon. As he spoke, he felt a weird sensation at the back of his mouth; it felt as if one of his teeth were loose.

It had got much darker in the wood. The sun had not yet set but the sky had clouded over. The two kids had lost all track of time. Emily peered at Simon in the gloom.

"You have a black eye." She remarked sadly.

"At the very least." Said Simon grimly.

"Are you going to report them?"

"I don't think there's any point, do you?"

52

Bernice heard Simon come in late that Sunday afternoon, but she was in the bathroom and didn't see him. Peter was lying on his bed. Simon called to his mum that he was going to have an early night and shut his door with a decisive click.

Bernice thought that was a bit strange, he had sounded a bit odd as if his speech was distorted, but she didn't think much of it. She was preoccupied with her thoughts on Alex and Peter, both.

It was only the following morning after Peter had left for work, as Bernice was pottering around the kitchen, that Simon, having cleaned himself up as much as he was able, entered the kitchen wincing. Except for his mouth which felt swollen, and the obvious black eye, the worst of his injuries were hidden beneath his clothes.

Simon's ribs were killing him, whether they were cracked or merely bruised he couldn't tell, but they made breathing painful; he could not inhale properly. His lower back was a mass of kaleidoscopic bruising. Although he had been expecting it to be bad, he had been shocked to see in the mirror, how terrible it actually was. Whether due to that or some other injury, he found difficulty in straightening one of his legs and limped into the kitchen.

Bernice, who had been drying dishes stopped what she was doing and turned to stare at him in horror. Her arms dropped to her sides limply, still gripping a mug and a tea towel.

"What the…!" Who did this to you?" Almost immediately, tears sprung to her eyes. She knew instinctively that this was not the result of a fair fight, that Simon had not been at fault, had not deserved this beating. Bernice knew this, not because she harboured delusions about the superior character of her offspring, but because she had seen them all yesterday exactly for what they were; cold-hearted and mean-spirited and she knew that they were more than capable of this kind of brutality, in fact it sat shining within them, the cruelty, just beneath their thick, ignorant skins.

In the kitchen that day, Bernice cried in pity for Simon and for herself and even for Peter, for the fact that they had come to this godforsaken place in order to be bullied mercilessly and mistreated. Simon did not cry. He had cried in the night and felt worse for it. Crying seemed to use up the energy that he needed to deal with the onslaught of pain.

It took a while for Bernice's hysteria to die down. Simon sat patiently at the kitchen table and waited. There was no point in talking until she was calmer, and when she did, eventually sit opposite him, her face swollen with the crying and still shaking, Simon told her exactly what had happened. He included the build up to the event itself, the bullying, the misery on the bus, the friendship with Emily. In his strange new voice (because he could not open his mouth fully), he didn't leave anything out.

Bernice listened with fury radiating through her, but also aware that she had to look after Simon now, that she was the adult in this situation, and it was up to her to get him medical care.

"We need to get you to Cavershall, to the hospital, and to a dentist probably."

Simon had no intention of arguing with that.

"How? Dad has the car?"

"Oh!" Bernice immediately felt hysteria rising in her. It was true, they did not have a car, there was no taxi service in that terrible village.

"We can call dad, tell him to come back and get us?"

"No!" An idea was coming to Bernice, in small increments, she wanted to make them squirm, all of them, as a collective.

Simon didn't yet see it like that. He didn't yet lump all the villagers together. His wrath was directed, at that moment, only towards Gary and his cronies.

"What do you mean no?"

"Your dad will be in meetings all day, I doubt we'll be able to get hold of him in any case. I have an idea."

Even through his pain, Simon realised his mum was being weird, there was a strange unhinged lilt to her tone of voice which he had never heard before.

53

Sarah had once given Bernice her number, before when things had seemed kinder. Sarah picked up the phone immediately as if she was sitting next to it, and in her heightened nervous state, Bernice jolted in her seat.

Without preamble she told Sarah that Simon had been attacked by some boys in his class and that he needed to go to hospital in Cavershall to see a doctor.

"I used to be a nurse, maybe I…"

"He needs a doctor and a dentist." Bernice stated firmly, barely recognising the new cold authority in her voice.

There was an uncomfortable pause, some distant muted conferring to be heard from Sarah's end and then she came back onto the line, sounding uncertain.

"Jacob is here and happy to drive you."

"Thank you." Bernice replied curtly, "We will wait in front of the house."

Simon had got the gist of the conversation and told Bernice that he found Jacob creepy.

"They're all creepy." Stated Bernice, she felt, almost by stealth a new steeliness and clarity dominate her thoughts. "You don't have to talk to him, we are using him for a lift, that's all."

Jacob pulled up ten minutes later in quite an expensive car. Simon had been interested in cars as a young teen, and recognised this as a fancy one. Without preamble and without saying anything, Simon got in the back and Bernice into the passenger side.

"Erm hello." Jacob looked anxious and dishevelled and far younger than his years. He clearly lacked the bluster of either of his parents, or so it seemed. Yet, Bernice recalled that she had thought Sarah shy and good-natured and that had turned out to be a completely deceptive facade.

"There's a hospital in Cavershall. We'll go directly there." She stated, without returning Jacob's greeting.

Simon, even through his pain, was a bit shocked at how impolite his mum was being, he had never seen her like that before, so brusque and cold.

"Sure, yes!" Jacob seemed anxious to be agreeable and as the miles fled by, and the heavy silence in the car became ever more oppressive, Simon almost pitied him. Bernice, in the front seat, kept her head upright and rigid as if she had to stay alert and cross, even here on this long, boring drive.

Simon had the impression then, that Jacob was not an aggressor, was not fully one of 'them.' He seemed weak and insubstantial, his grey eyes watery and pathetic. Even though his mother had made her stance clear, Simon felt the urge to talk to Jacob, if only to render the atmosphere in the car a bit more normal and relaxed.

"I heard you just returned from seminary, how was that? Is it like university?" His broken tooth clicked weirdly and his own voice sounded strange.

Bernice bristled in the front seat but didn't comment.

Jacob caught Simon's eye briefly in the rearview mirror. His hands were tense on the steering wheel.

"It was…yeah, kind of like university, I guess. Probably less fun!" He attempted a weak chuckle. It wasn't convincing, more a show of nerves than humour.

The silence returned, as heavily as before, but Simon still felt compelled to dispel the awkwardness.

"What will you do now then?"

"I guess, I…well, I'm supposed to take over from my dad eventually, and until then, I have to…I mean, I want to organise the Friday youth club."

Involuntarily, Simon shuddered, in his head they all lined up, those brutal youths, waiting to punch him.

"What else? I mean, that's just Friday evening, what do you do the rest of the time?"

"I still study, our church more specifically. There's a great deal behind the running of the church, I mean the economics of it…"

"The economics of it?" Bernice's head swivelled round. "What do you mean?" Already, she was beginning to understand how it worked.

54

Even after the firemen had secured the building and the damaged machine had been removed, Peter had to stay many hours in the office in terse discussions with the rest of the management team about the protocol post fire hazard and endure lengthy debates about how long the factory needed to stay shut in order that all machines be inspected in case of a similar issue.

The entire time, he was thinking about the absence of Samantha and Dennis and fretting that the two were related.

The rest of the management team were still talking, even though it was past 8pm, when Peter told them that he did not feel well and had to leave. It was quite a convincing excuse, as it happened, because he did seem exceptionally pale and sweaty in the harsh overhead light of the conference room.

As soon as he left the building, Peter jumped into his car and headed towards Tensit, driving too fast and too erratically for the narrow country roads. Most did not have street lights and it was only the sudden glare of a headlight which would alert one to on-coming traffic. As he drove, he felt the rapid, uncomfortable hammering of his heart against his ribs. He was relieved, in Tensit, to see the lights glaring in the ugly terraced house where he knew Samantha lived.

Peter was further relieved when Samantha opened the door to him. He had knocked with his knuckles rather than use the electronic bell; somehow it seemed too late for that. She opened the door slowly and cautiously. He noticed that she was still wearing the same beige, unflattering dress that she had been wearing that day in the office. It seemed a long time ago that she had suggested that they make an appointment to chat, and in fact, now she was looking at him in bewilderment and almost fear, as if she couldn't work out why Peter was there and what he wanted with her.

"Peter!" She exclaimed.

"Can we chat now? Do you have time?" He realised that he sounded both pleading and somehow peevish.

"Peter, you don't look well. I…"

"Can I come in?"

"Yes, yes, I suppose so."

Samantha ushered him into the small kitchen. It was brightly lit with fluorescent bulbs overhead, and the remains of a meal for two littered the cheap table. Peter had been in that room before, but just to grab a glass of water. It was a cramped and shoddy space, the harsh lighting contributing to the discomfort of it.

Without preamble Samantha transferred the dirty dishes into the sink. Her skin, in that light, appeared jaundiced and Peter imagined that his did too. He listened out for sounds of the flatmate but couldn't hear anything.

"I think she's gone to bed." Samantha stated flatly, as if reading his mind. "It is quite late after all."

"Well..." Peter thought that it was about 9pm by then, hardly that late. "Sorry. I looked for you when the alarm went off but you had gone."

"Yes." She seemed a bit sheepish then, a light blush rose in her pale cheeks. "I know it was a bit naughty, but I took the opportunity to leave."

"I don't care about it being naughty, but we had an appointment!" Peter struggled to keep the anguish out of his voice.

"Yes, yes, I know Peter, I'm sorry. We can talk now." Samantha said gently, as if she was placating him.

55

Bernice made Jacob drop her and Simon off at the door of Accident and Emergency. She was very relieved that Cavershall hospital even had an A&E, it was by no means a given. She told Jacob, in her new uncompromising voice, that he would have to park somewhere and wait for them. He looked a bit shocked but nodded dumbly. He seemed intimidated by Bernice, and Simon, despite the pain he was in, felt a glimmer of pride. He hadn't seen his mum like that in a long time, not since they had lived in London, certainly.

As a minor, Simon was moved straight through to the paediatric department. There were very few patients in A&E or indeed visible anywhere. The hospital was old and had clearly not been renovated for many years. The corridors were low-ceilinged and the orange bulbs overhead hummed. Simon felt the buzzing and the ubiquitous chemical hospital smell seep unpleasantly into his nervous system.

The nurses however, and the young doctor that Simon got to see remarkably quickly, were friendly and concerned in a professional, detached medical way. It was established immediately, via X-ray, that a couple of Simon's ribs were broken and that his tooth had been dislodged but the root would still have to be removed. Beyond that, all his injuries were 'just' bruises, however serious they felt.

On the way to the dental department, Simon and Bernice were accompanied by the young doctor and subjected to a light interrogation. Simon told the man that he had got into a scrape at school and his lie wasn't questioned. The doctor merely said "Aha" in a disinterested sort of way.

All along that endless corridor, however, Simon waited, tense, almost with bated breath, for his mother to launch into the real reason for his injuries, but, surprisingly, she remained silent, her mouth set in a thin tight line.

It was not until three hours later that Simon and Bernice emerged from the hospital. A heavy grey sky hung over the town and a bright frost nipped the air. Simon's face was swollen from where the root of his tooth had been removed. He had been prescribed strong painkillers and he had taken one immediately as the packet was passed over from the hospital pharmacy. He was feeling pleasantly fuzzy. Jacob was where they had left him, waiting in the car. He had the radio on and was listening to old-fashioned rock music. This seemed strange to Simon, although he couldn't have said why, and, as high as he was, everything felt strange at that moment.

Jacob smiled at them anxiously when they returned to the car. He asked Simon how he felt and made no comment about the hours that he had sat there waiting. Simon wondered if he had gone anywhere to have a snack or use the toilet, but there was something about the pinched expression on Jacob's face that told him that he had just sat there waiting. Jacob was one of those people, the thought came clearly to Simon then, who just do exactly as they are told.

Simon dozed during the drive home and had vivid, technicolour dreams. He understood then why people became drug addicts, what the point of it was. He felt as if nothing really mattered, as if he was floating. It felt wonderful.

Bernice stared out the window in silence. At some point the rain started lashing down, and the sophisticated windscreen wipers, front and back, swished back and forth in time with the music playing softly on the radio.

It was still the old-fashioned rock songs.

56

"I do think Linda is stalking you," Stated one of the boys. "I keep seeing her near the English department."

The four friends were sitting in Tina's room. Three of them were squashed up on her single bed, and the boy who was talking was sitting on her chair with his legs crossed in a yoga pose. Both boys studied dance as one of their modules and were more flexible than they looked.

"She is not!" Said Poppy, rolling her eyes and accepting a cigarette from Tina. "The psychology department is literally next door to my one…and I know she has to go there all the time, she studies in their library!"

"Hmmm, if you say so."

"I don't know, he might be right you know, I see her a lot, skulking around," Commented Tina, "More than I feel I should."

"That's only because you're all looking out for her now! None of you even knew who she was before, so obviously you wouldn't have noticed her!"

Poppy struggled not to get impatient with her new friends and their predilection for drama. The room was dense with the fug of cigarette smoke and the heat of all their bodies and the overpowering musty odour of their semi-dirty clothes.

"Hopefully, you'll move in here after Christmas anyway, or into another one of the halls. It would be great to have you nearby, and not sharing our beds, I mean!" Laughed Tina.

"That's the plan." Sighed Poppy. She was doubtful it would happen though. For her to move in anywhere, it would mean that someone had to move out, effectively drop out of university.

"People drop out all the time!" Stated Tina confidently, eerily as if she was reading Poppy's mind. "They get homesick, they can't cope, they have family problems, all sorts of things…"

"Hmmm." Poppy thought about her family then. She was worried about them. The village sounded like a nightmare and she had the impression that they were not telling her all of it, all there was to know. Probably so as not to scare her away. She understood that they missed her which was lovely in its way, but Poppy would have preferred to be appraised of the truth as to what was going on, all the gritty details.

Even Simon, who could usually be relied upon to be honest with her, was being unusually reticent. He had told her, the other day, that he had been involved in a skirmish with some of the boys in his class and that they had knocked out his tooth.

"A 'skirmish'?" Poppy had countered sceptically, "That sounds like quite a bit more than that!"

"It's fine, honestly. I don't want to think about it or talk about it. When are you coming home?" Poppy could hear the tension in Simon's voice, even down the phone line.

"Term doesn't end until mid-December, so then I guess?"

"Oh." Simon sighed loudly.

"Surely you'll have school until then anyway?"

"Hm, yeah, I guess." Simon sounded quiet then, defeated. "I fucking hate that school." He exclaimed suddenly, with a glimmer of strange fury.

Poppy was taken aback. Her brother had never hated school. He had never been a geek or one of the super cool kids, but he was always popular enough, and bright enough to enjoy all his subjects without issue. She tried to get him to elaborate then, but he just seemed to shut down. His answers to her questions became monosyllabic, and soon Poppy had no choice but to give up.

57

"I am pregnant." Stated Samantha. She was sitting opposite Peter at that awful little table in her kitchen and regarding him with pity. Somewhere a clock ticked, except for that a silence settled on them both as heavy as a blanket, and Peter had the odd sensation that he was being suffocated.

Before he even asked the question, a part of him knew the answer and yet, inevitably, he asked it anyway.

"It's not mine, is it?"

Sorrowfully, Samantha shook her head.

"Although, that wouldn't have made things any easier, not really."

"Yes, it would!" Peter protested, anguished, "I would have left Bernice, we could have…"

"No." Samantha stated with surprising firmness, "It would never have worked and now it definitely won't. I was trying to stay away from you, as a kindness."

"A kindness!" He stared at her, incredulous. In the ugly light, both of the seemed aged and haggard. "You get pregnant by Dennis…" Peter spat out the name with repugnance, "and then avoid me! There was no kindness in any of that, none that I can see…"

"It wasn't my choice!" It was Samantha's turn to seem incredulous, the pink colour in her cheeks intensified. "I am shocked that you haven't got it yet! He raped me! several times! In the toilets at work! That time I told you that I stubbed my toe, he was trying to grab me again and…"

Of course, deep down, Peter had known that already. Not the repellent details but the gist. He had reacted to the threat of Dennis by trying to get him removed, without realising that the crime had already taken place; it was a fait accompli.

Peter felt tears sting his eyes and then trickle down his cheeks. Too little, too late. The phrase entered his head unbidden. He had been powerless to protect Samantha. He hadn't even realised the extent of the threat. Dennis in the conference room, licking his thin lips, waiting for an opportunity, calculating. Peter hadn't watched him closely enough, he had merely sat there worrying about cheating on Bernice, the complications of it, like a middle-aged fool, while the hunter had already ensnared Samantha in his trap. He felt great pity for her but more for himself, still. He reached across the table in order to lay one hand onto her arm, but she jerked her body backwards, stiffly.

"I think you should leave now." She said sadly but firmly.

"What will you do?"

"I'll hand in my notice, for now. I can't stand being anywhere near Dennis."

"Does he know?"

"I don't think so, unless…well, I'm sure there are rumours and he will have heard them, but I haven't spoken to him."

Peter nodded. He felt a terrible exhaustion suddenly. He pictured himself standing and moving, using his legs to walk out of that ugly house and into his car. He imagined the cold steering wheel beneath his hands and he couldn't bear the thought of that sequence of events, of any of it.

Samantha was still watching him but she had already left his life. She had left it weeks ago without him realising.

58

Simon dozed in the car, dopey and drugged, half woke to stumble into the house and up the stairs and then fell asleep properly, deeply, and immediately on his bed, fully clothed.

Jacob was not expecting thanks and was even surprised that Bernice said goodbye. During the silent journey home, he had wondered exactly what his parents had done to cause Bernice's coldness. He knew that they, personally, hadn't beaten Simon up. He somewhat grudgingly admired her attitude though. Jacob himself was too afraid to stand up to his own parents and always had been.

Bernice, herself exhausted, went into Simon's room, removed his shoes, and covered him with a thick blanket. He was lying on his stomach, snoring with his mouth partially open. He smelt sour, of hospitals and chemicals.

Bernice wasn't hungry in the slightest but forced herself to eat some toast, stuffing it into her mouth without tasting it. It stuck drily to the roof of her mouth. She then went to sit in the rapidly darkening living room. She watched the shadows take over completely as minutes then hours passed. She didn't switch on the lights. The silence fell thickly over her. She wondered how she, how they, had got there, how it had come to this?

When Peter eventually came in, hours later, directly from Samantha's house, Bernice was lying on the sofa asleep, her legs pulled up underneath her. Peter watched her from the doorway. He felt, once again, the overwhelming compulsion to cry. He had been crying on and off during the entire drive back to Constance from Tensit, the tears blurring his vision on the road; it was something of a miracle that he had made it back in one piece. He cried for Samantha and for himself. He cried with impotent fury and had vivid visions of finding Dennis, of tracking him down and attacking him, of wiping his stupid smug expression of his face. It should be easy enough to find his address, he imagined. It would involve a quick trip to the HR office at the factory, a made-up excuse.

Peter was still thinking all these things, they were whirling round his brain incessantly, unpleasantly, he felt as if he was on some kind of hideous fairground ride that he couldn't get off. There was a tension in his chest, a weight. He was standing in the dark doorway of the living room, watching unseeing the sleeping silhouette of his wife.

Bernice stirred and woke.

"We have to talk." She said to Peter, alert immediately with the same adrenalin that had been pumping through her all day.

"Why?" Peter felt fearful and confused, was this about Samantha? How could Bernice possibly know about that?

She sat up straight on the sofa and Peter could see her eyes glinting in the murky dark. Some metres from their house a streetlamp shone, weak glimmers of light entered the room stealthily, like thieves.

"Simon was attacked by some boys from his school yesterday at that stupid picnic." She informed Peter without preamble.

"But…when? We were there?"

Bernice scoffed. "You were barely there and I left soon after. We didn't see him when he came home last night which is on both of us…"

"How…"

"He's fine, well physically he's going to be OK. We went to the hospital in Cavershall today. He lost a tooth and he's got a couple of broken ribs…but, Peter, we have got to leave this fucking place! We can't stay here!"

Peter collapsed into the stiff armchair opposite her and lowered his head into his hands.

"I would love to get out of here, but what about my job? If I leave suddenly now, it will cause them massive inconvenience and they will not give me a good reference. Effectively, I will be blacklisted, no one will give me a job! We can't both be unemployed!"

"We'll manage!"

"Come on! Be realistic! We still have a huge mortgage on our house in London and now apparently it has all these issues that need fixing. It would have helped enormously to rent it out, but as it is…we're broke, is the bottom line, and without a job or even a decent reference, well…"

All that was true, Bernice knew, and yet she was overcome by an emotion akin to despair, a fervent desire to escape that awful village, almost as if it was literally keeping the Jensons captive. The only small consolation was that both her and Peter seemed united in their visceral hate of Constance and its inhabitants.

59

Poppy was beginning to think that Tina and the boys may have a point. Initially sceptical of what she considered to be their paranoia, she had begun to feel, quite often when she walked through campus, as if she was being followed.

This was despite talking to herself quite firmly and telling herself that the idea of someone following her was only even in her head because her friends kept scaring her. There was no rational behind it. If, in fact, Linda was following her, what would even be the point? What would she hope to achieve by doing so?

The boys would say that it was an intimidation tactic, and when they said things like that, Poppy would scoff; but now she wasn't so sure they were wrong, at least not completely. Often, when walking alone, she would sense a presence behind her, she would suddenly feel an uncomfortable shiver run through her, but then, when she turned around, sharply, there would be no one there.

By that point, Poppy had removed the vast majority of her belongings from her bedsit and they were all stacked haphazardly in her friends' rooms. Poppy had taken to climbing up the concrete fire escape stairs to get to their rooms, in order to avoid the scrutiny of the managers in the halls of residence. Fortunately, they were busy, at that time, with some particularly unruly behaviour on behalf of some members of the university rugby team, so they were distracted.

The night descended quickly in November. The university campus, so verdant and appealing during bright daylight hours, quickly became shadowy and sinister as the light faded. There were lampposts, of course, but they were not particularly close together, and between them dense foliage and wooded areas provided multiple possibilities to hide and stalk. Of course, there were often many other students, mostly walking in groups also navigating those same shadowy paths. Poppy always tried to attach herself to people when she knew she had to walk through the campus after dark, but for various reasons, that was not possible all the time.

It so happened that it was mid- November and Poppy was walking through the campus park after her last lecture had finished, a little after 6pm. A brisk wind was causing the trees to sway and the leaves to rustle.

Poppy drew her arms tightly across her chest. That morning, she had underestimated the weather and the jacket that she was wearing was not padded enough for the onslaught of bitterly cold air that seeped under her clothes.

Poppy was deep in thought about an essay which was overdue but which she hadn't started yet, and initially did not even hear the footsteps quickening behind her. The wind, in any case, was so all-pervasive that it obliterated and deadened all other sounds.

By the time she did hear and react, the shock caused a physical pain to throb in her chest, and just like her father, so far away, for one fleeting panicked second, as she turned, she wondered if she was having a heart attack, if it was all over for her.

Poppy swung round on the path, wielding her heavy backpack in one hand, ready to use it as a weapon.

The figure behind her instinctively brought their arms up to shield their face.

60

Simon spent weeks at home recovering from his injuries whilst his parents agonised about what to do. Peter still went to work and moved through his days like a sluggish zombie, on autopilot. Samantha had handed in her notice, but also called in sick, so Peter understood that she had every intention of spending her notice period at home, away from him and Dennis.

Despite everything, despite the permanent physical lovesick ache in his heart, he was relieved that Samantha was away from Dennis, and the urge to attack Dennis himself never left him. All day Peter would navigate the sterile-looking rooms and the corridors of the factory with his fists so tightly clenched that his nails left indentations in his palms.

Dennis, as if somehow sensing that he was in danger, was rarely spotted. Only occasionally, on the other side of a huge room, invariably laughing with someone, his dry, filthy chuckle would bridge the distant between them, and Peter would feel the desire for violence leap in him, so strong that it was almost impossible to quash.

Bernice, left alone with Simon would rarely leave the house. Those initial days, when he was still weakened and poorly, brought to mind their first days as a family in Constance and struggling to adjust to that uncomfortable cottage. The pair moved from stiff kitchen chair to uncomfortable sofa, trying and failing to find relief for their cramped limbs. Simon and his mother watched TV and played cards and boardgames. Outside the November sky hung grim and darkly grey and night swung over Constance suddenly and immediately in the late afternoons just like a curtain swooping down.

In the evenings, when Simon retired to his room, (Bernice had bought him his own television in there, she was willing to do anything, right then, to make him feel better), Peter would return and the pair would argue in low agonised whispers about how much they wanted to get away from Constance and what they could realistically do given their financial situation.

By the time that Alex called Bernice, she was amazed to realise that with all the drama, she had almost forgotten about him. When she heard his voice however, she could not deny to herself that her initial reaction was relief. Alex had nothing to do with any of this, he was, ergo, both a welcome distraction and an even more welcome reminder of Bernice's much missed life in London. Just to hear his voice was to pretend to herself that the Jensons were still there in their suburb, blissfully ignorant of the existence of Constance. Bernice had completely forgotten, by then, that she had ever been unhappy there, or if she remembered suddenly, she would rationalise that it was never London as a place which made her miserable, but rather the circumstances of her life there; her marriage or her job.

In any case, now that Alex was once again summoning her, she wanted to go to him. Like an owner he was, calling his faithful dog. Deep down, Bernice knew this and yet she wanted to see him all the same.

Alex and Bernice agreed to meet in the same café in Cavershall where they had met before, and by the time Peter returned from work, looking as exhausted and defeated as he always did, Bernice was already thinking of the lie to tell him so that she could borrow the car.

Peter barely noticed Bernice when he entered the house. He had endured an unpleasant, and somewhat mystifying, telling off from his boss in London on the telephone.

The man, who was the one who had promoted Peter and was the reason Peter was now manager of this factory in the arse end of nowhere, told Peter that he had been receiving complaints about his conduct from various reliable sources, 'people' were apparently saying that he was permanently distracted and incompetent in his role.

"Complaints? Various reliable sources?" Peter was shocked but at the same time somehow unsurprised. In his mind's eye he saw Dennis's smug, cold-eyed expression. Was it not enough that he had destroyed Samantha's life? Now, apparently, he wanted to destroy Peter's too.

Almost, almost Peter didn't have the energy to argue, though. He felt so tired, so terribly exhausted. He just wanted to lie down somewhere comfortable and cover his head with a pillow. He couldn't though. He had his children to think of, and his wife too, such as she was. He still needed to provide for all of them, well, Simon certainly and he still needed to pay the mortgage of their London house.

61

Bernice and Alex met in the same café in Cavershall that they had met in last time, as arranged. Bernice had told Peter that she needed the car to see the dentist again for a follow-up appointment, and they both knew that she was lying. She had told the same lie to Simon who had been slumped listlessly on his bed staring blankly at the TV. He had nodded his head, but he hadn't been listening. He had been entrenched deep in his thoughts, as he always was these days.

This time, the illicit couple spent very little time in the café before retreating to Alex's hotel.

Bernice had been more silent and less friendly than usual and Alex had perceived that as a challenge, but she had not resisted his advances as he might have expected, in fact she had welcomed them. He found that slightly baffling but naturally, he didn't complain.

The hotel room had the blandness of most other hotel rooms, even the same mass-laundry smell, innocuous. They could have been in any hotel anywhere, the whole situation seemed farcical in its banality. Bernice felt deep within herself a fury which manifested in extreme restlessness. She didn't know what to do with herself, so she might as well do this; that was what she thought. It was an escape of sorts, a distraction anyway.

It was when Bernice and Alex were leaving the hotel that Bernice spotted a familiar figure on the pavement before them. It was a large woman, sporting an oversized floral, full-length dress, and a shapeless beige coat. Sarah narrowed her eyes at Bernice and then let her gaze settle on Alex, a small, cruel smile playing about her lips. As a couple, the pair were not touching and yet it was obvious that they had just left the hotel together and conclusions could inevitably be drawn.

Bernice didn't react, did not even give Sarah the satisfaction of acknowledging her, and yet a glimmer of fear wormed its way through her. She recalled only too clearly Sarah's garbled threat at the barbecue, something about knowing important people at the factory, an implication that she and her hideous husband were not as provincial and harmless as they may have seemed at first sight.

Bernice was distracted that afternoon in her dealings with Alex and that came across as indifference. This made Bernice more attractive to him not less. It was frustrating to Alex that she was no longer needy and clingy, and he found himself being more charming than usual in order to reel her back in. After their rendezvous at the hotel and after the sighting of Sarah, Alex insisted that they go for a drink. Alex didn't know, incidentally, that Bernice had seen Sarah and what that meant, and she never told him. He had nothing to do with any of it; he was but a tourist.

Bernice reluctantly agreed to a drink, although she would rather have gone home. Her lie about the dentist was more and more obvious the longer she stayed out, although she suspected, correctly, that nobody cared. The pub they went to, the first one they stumbled upon, was depressingly typical of a rundown small town in the way the café wasn't and Bernice felt, weirdly, as if it was somehow more appropriate, more fitting, there in that location. The quirky, cool café had felt like an anomaly. It didn't belong there. It was too fancy, too sophisticated and fashionable for the likes of Cavershall.

Bernice needed, somehow, for all the trappings of her new hated life to be negative. The filthy pub with its stench of unwashed people, spilt beer and decades of burnt tobacco was exactly as bad as she wanted it to be.

62

Victor cowered before Poppy, still covering his face with his spindly black-clad arms.

"What the hell?" Fumed Poppy struggling to catch her breath, "What the hell do you think you are doing? You were supposed to have left ages ago!"

"I stayed longer…I decided not to go to university this year." Victor panted. Tentatively, he lowered his arms from his face. Poppy maintained her distance, still not trusting him. She was gratified to notice a large, boisterous group of students approaching along the same path.

"Yeah, but why are you following me and creeping up behind me?"

"No…I…I didn't mean to scare you, I just wanted to talk, I saw you and…"

"You saw me and followed me!"

"Well, yes, but not in the dangerous way that you think!"

Poppy peered at him in the gloom. She walked on a bit, further down the path, and uncertainly, Victor followed. In the half-light of the next street light, he seemed pallid and harmless. Still clad in black, he had, nevertheless toned down the goth look and now just looked like an underfed boy with a penchant for wearing dark clothes.

"But why are you here?" Poppy persisted, "In the university campus park?"

"It's a pretty park," Victor remarked feebly, "I just came to have a walk and then I saw you…"

"Hmmm…"

It was plausible, Poppy thought. It was an attractive, popular park, that was true, and open to the public. However, the sky was darkening rapidly by then, was it realistic that anyone would choose dusk to appreciate a 'pretty park,' as Victor called it? Even if he was unthreatening, and he did seem it, Poppy still didn't want anything to do with Victor. She hadn't wanted to hang out with him before and she didn't now, nothing had changed. Poppy was polite by nature, though, underneath her edgy exterior and she didn't want to be rude to Victor then. He seemed an object of pity, rather than anything more sinister. She felt impatience as she continued to walk in the direction of the university halls she unofficially squatted in. Victor trailed just behind her. Poppy found his continued presence disconcerting and unnerving if no longer actually scary.

"You shouldn't have crept up behind me, that was not cool."

Beside her, she sensed him nodding rapidly in agreement.

"I know that now. I made a mistake, sorry!"

The path which led to the hall her friends lived in was approaching, a turn off to the right. Poppy's pace quickened and she was relieved to realise that Victor was hanging back.

"I'm going down here now, bye!" She turned rapidly and strode off down the path.

"Bye!" He replied in a sorrowful voice, and Poppy felt slightly guilty, and then immediately afterwards annoyed with herself for feeling that way, she didn't owe Victor anything.

Tina was in her room when Poppy returned and immediately launched into an elaborate description of a costume she was planning on wearing to a fancy dress party at the student union bar. Poppy had been planning on telling her how Victor had approached her on campus, but the timing seemed off somehow, the mood wrong.

63

Simon was left alone in the house the day that Bernice went to the 'dentist' in Cavershall. It was just before midday, and having recovered physically, almost completely, Simon felt restless and bored. Had he not felt so antsy, he would certainly not have been tempted to answer the door when he heard the knocking.

His bullies would be in school at that time, Simon reasoned and there was nothing else concrete to fear, or so he thought. Jacob stood there, looking fragile and pallid, the same insipid hue as the colourless sky behind him. He smiled nervously at Simon, revealing crooked yellowish teeth and explained that he had popped over to see how he was.

Having been inside for so long, Simon stood in the doorway blinking rapidly against the onslaught of the bright light. It distracted him so that he took a while to reply and the silence between them was, for a long second, heavy.

"Come in!" Simon finally said, remembering his manners, and as Jason walked past him, Simon noticed that he was wearing the same weird old-fashioned suit that they all wore when they went to church. It crossed Simon's mind that the suit was a kind of uniform of sorts for them all. Jacob or the clothes he was wearing, smelt stale, as if he was preserved somewhere in mothballs. The smell followed him in and settled on the air.

In the kitchen, Jacob sat on one of the uncomfortable chairs and peered around skittishly, almost fearfully, but with apparent fascination. For the first time, Simon wondered what the interior of Jacob's house looked like, what it would be like to have Robert and Sarah as parents. Not great, he imagined, he shuddered slightly and filled the kettle in the sink. The running water cascaded loudly into the silence. Simon began to regret asking Jacob in almost immediately, it all seemed too awkward and he couldn't be bothered to be polite for the sake of it.

"I'm sorry for what happened to you." Jacob blurted out. He had his hands tightly clasped in front of him on the kitchen table and his tone seemed pinched and anxious.

"That's OK, it wasn't your fault. There are bullies everywhere."

"Oh, I know that, I know!" Agreed Jacob fervently, and Simon turned sharply to look at him.

"Were there bullies in your college too?" He asked.

Jacob lowered his head to stare at his hands and Simon couldn't help but notice that the top of his head, the hair there, was greasy. He felt a passing glimmer of revulsion.

"As you said," He was hanging his head and speaking into his chest, "They are everywhere, bullies I mean."

There was something not quite right about Jacob, Simon saw that clearly then. It was not surprising that he had been targeted, probably in all schools. In church, he would be protected to an extent; Robert was scary, even Sarah. Schools, however…they were lawless places.

"How did you get on with the high school in Tensit when you were there?"

Jacob glanced up at Simon with his huge grey eyes.

"God, but that place was awful!"

"Worse than the Seminary?"

"No, not worse, because…well, I was stuck in the Seminary, I couldn't leave!"

Jacob's voice was rising into an impassioned screech, he seemed increasingly disturbed, and Simon regretted starting this conversation. He had enough of his own problems.

"You must be relieved to be home." He said smoothly, trying to adopt a calming tone and nudging the cup of tea towards Jacob.

"Sort of" replied Jacob glumly. "I have to run this youth club on Fridays, it's really not my thing."

"No," Simon agreed, "I imagine it wouldn't be."

64

Simon wondered about Emily a great deal during those long boring days at home once he felt better. Probably because he didn't have much to do and because he was a fifteen-year-old boy, she popped up a great deal in his fantasies. He presumed that her parents had realised that she had sneaked off with him into the woods on that day and she had got into trouble because of it. He didn't know that for sure, however, until she called him, early in the evening the day after Jacob had visited.

Bernice had picked up the phone when it rang, but distracted ever since returning from the 'dentist,' she had passed the receiver over to Simon without a word.

"Are you OK? I wanted to call you before but my mum is watching me constantly!" Emily sounded breathless.

"They caught you then? At the barbecue?"

"Yes, one of their friends saw me go off with you and told them."

Simon snorted. "I bet they all know that Gary and his little crew beat me up too."

"They do know, I think. Even Miss Sanchez asked about you."

"She did?" Simon felt oddly touched.

"You didn't report him though, did you? Why not? That little shit has been allowed to get away with stuff for way too long!"

"It wouldn't have made any difference. He would have said it was a fair fight, all his goons would have backed him up."

"Hmmm, that's true, I suppose, all his little bastard friends would back him for sure, they always do." Emily sighed heavily down the line. "I'm grounded you know, until Christmas."

Simon couldn't help thinking that Emily was barely ever allowed out anyway, that it wouldn't make a great deal of difference to her life, but he made sympathetic noises.

"I'm only allowed to school…yippee!...and church."

"What about Friday youth club at church?" Asked Simon, a plan taking shape in his mind.

"Yeah, I heard that's starting, this week, I think."

"Would they allow you to go to that?" Simon persisted. He could picture Emily clearly as she spoke, her wide eyes, long slim neck. Desire came to him suddenly and acutely. He felt more alert than he had done since the attack and slightly desperate.

"Why would we want to go to that?" Emily was a bit slow on the uptake. "Jacob is…weird. He always has been."

"To see each other!" Simon exclaimed, a bit impatiently. "We could just use the youth club as an excuse!"

"Right, of course!"

"What do you mean by Jacob being weird? I mean, I realise that, it's obvious, but you've known him way longer than I have."

"I wouldn't say I know him, yeah I've seen him around all my life, maybe with his awful parents in church, but he's so much older than us, and honestly, I can't remember ever having spoken to him. It's his dad that really gives me the creeps to be honest with you, I always make sure I stay as far away from Robert as physically possible."

"So, what would you say is wrong with him?"

"With which one?"

"With either, with both!"

"I think that Jacob has 'special needs' as Miss Sanchez calls it" Emily used a slightly mocking tone when she said 'special needs' which Simon chose to ignore.

"Right." He said bluntly, "What about Robert?"

"He's just really creepy!"

"I know, but anything else? I mean, anything concrete?"

"Rumours, I guess…in villages like this there are always rumours, but honestly most of them are too bizarre to be believable."

65

Peter had a new secretary sitting where Samantha used to sit. She was an older lady, June, with a neat grey bob. She had a tranquillity about her and a great efficiency, and Peter, in those days, when his mind was in permanent turmoil, felt an immense gratitude for her existence. Without June organising his days, he felt it doubtful that he would have been able to function at all, never mind work.

It wasn't only that Peter's mind felt as if it was permanently stuck in turbulence, so that he struggled to concentrate on anything, it also seemed to him that his depression was rapidly becoming a physical issue as well.

He felt exhausted in his bones, every day. He felt as if he was dragging his unwilling carcass through time, it ached constantly. There was a permanent heaviness in his chest or on his chest, as if someone had deposited a large stone there and it was weighing him down. When Peter mentioned his physical issues, particularly the dull pain in his chest, to Bernice, she would tell him that it was psychosomatic, that his depression, and he was obviously depressed, was manifesting itself in bodily aches and pains.

At that time, Peter had no one to talk to but his wife. Simon when he faced him across the kitchen table, looked better in himself, but there was a strange distracted glint in his eye which Peter hoped was because of a girl and nothing more sinister.

To add to his physical malaise, Peter also felt that his performance at work was being scrutinized, that he was being watched at the exact time when he knew he was at his very worst. It was a terrible Catch 22. His colleagues seemed to pop into his office unannounced with strange frequency and Peter wondered if they had been sent to spy on him and judge his capability. When he mentioned this to Bernice, she scoffed and told him he was being paranoid, but, at the same time, he had the unnerving sensation that she wasn't really listening to him.

In the evenings Peter poured over bank statements and other financial documents pertaining to their mortgage, to try and work out whether there was any way that he could leave the factory and that the family could survive with him being unemployed and the answer was no. Not at all. They had got away with an interest only mortgage on their London townhouse for too long and just six months previously, that deal had come to an end and their repayments were now massive.

Bernice showed no interest in the documents that Peter perused in the evening at the kitchen table, and because of this too he felt a growing resentment towards her. Why couldn't she at least offer to get a job in Tensit or Cavershall? Why was the entire financial burden on him?

At night, he dreamt of Samantha. She would appear before him, heavily pregnant in the wide shapeless dresses she had worn in her last weeks at the factory. In his dreams, she seemed so real, that he often felt as if he could just reach out and touch her. Somehow, in a dreamscape, he would know that her baby was his. When he woke, agitated, and confused, he found that his hand would sometimes be resting on Bernice's shoulder. Occasionally, in her sleep, Bernice would turn towards Peter and he would feel the weight of the air that she breathed and a terrible disappointment that she was not Samantha.

66

Bernice ran into Sarah outside the shop in the village. It was nearly the end of November and on that morning, a bright frost sparkled all over the ground, the fields, and the buildings. It all looked, thought Bernice cynically, deceptively pretty.

Bernice was not paying attention, she was deep in thought about Alex who had called her the day before wanting to meet up again. Because she was not concentrating, she didn't manage to avoid Sarah as she had done of late. She had found, on several other occasions, that being attentive and observant had paid off.

Not this time, alas.

" Had fun in Cavershall, did you?" Sarah kept her tone deceptively pleasant but Bernice wasn't fooled and was not in the mood for whatever unpleasantness was doubtlessly forthcoming.

"I have no idea what you're talking about Sarah, what is it you want?"

"I wouldn't be rude and snappy if I were you, you don't know…"

"What don't I know, exactly?"

Bernice stared straight at Sarah's doughy face, she told herself that she was unafraid, that Sarah was a bully and bullies had to be faced, but at the same time, she felt her hands tremble and a shiver run down her back, and it wasn't just because of the cold she knew, she was wearing multiple layers.

"I don't think" Bernice watched Sarah's thin, pale lips enunciate each word carefully, "that you want to complicate Peter's life further. I have heard that he is already having a hard time of it."

Despite her determination to stand up to Sarah, Bernice felt her resolve wavering. It was creepy what this woman knew or thought she knew, it really did seem as if she had spies everywhere.

"Peter is just fine, thank you!" Bernice asserted through gritted teeth, but her voice emerged strangely squeaky.

"OK, OK!" Sarah laughed once, a barking laugh, her terrible teeth on full display. "I may just pop down to the factory to have a word. Did I mention we had friends there?"

"Do whatever you feel you must." Bernice tried to give Sarah a steely glance, but she felt her limbs shake involuntarily and there was a strange and unpleasant falling sensation in her stomach. She turned on her heel and left, trying to regulate her breathing.

What was Sarah even threatening? That she would tell Peter about Alex? That she would talk to whatever slimy contact she had at the factory and get him sacked? Perhaps, it was all a massive bluff, but to what end? What did Sarah want?

Bernice had meant to buy provisions for Simon and to go straight home, but now that plan had been interrupted and consequently abandoned. Bernice started walking, as she had done many times, alone across the crisp fields. She walked fast as if speed on its own could outmanoeuvre the turmoil of her own thoughts. They had to get out of there, that was for sure. That was all that she could think; no logical solutions, just panic. Her heart battered against her chest and she wondered if that was how Peter felt, but no, he seemed overcome with apathy and lethargy and she herself felt a great dizzying whirlwind of fear.

67

Simon told Jacob he would help him with his youth club and Jacob had been pathetically grateful. Even in that instance, Simon felt within him a mean and triumphant glimmer. You poor fool, he thought, do you not realise that it is obvious that I am using you?

"I won't let Gary come, we can ban him!" Jacob offered as if Simon needed further persuading.

"Great!" That was actually a relief. "Can you do that though?"

"I can try, I need to ask my dad."

"Right." Jacob sighed. That didn't seem very hopeful. He might well be stuck with physically avoiding Gary within a cramped space, when literally his only motivation for attending the youth club was the possibility of hanging out with Emily.

"What's the idea behind this youth club anyway?"

"Prayer and board games."

"Board games, OK," The two were on the phone but clearly Simon's scepticism was apparent in his voice.

"I know, I know." Jacob sighed. "This is all my dad's idea obviously, he wants me to get used to managing people." He laughed bitterly. "As if that's going to work with that lot!"

Simon felt sorry for Jacob then, on multiple levels. He pictured vividly the cold-eyed callousness of his former classmates, the cold-eyed callousness of Robert himself.

Of course it wasn't going to work.

"We may have to change the program a bit Jacob mate!"

Laughed Simon.

"You are welcome to run the whole thing as far as I'm concerned!"

"Definitely, no, I don't want to do that. But I'll be there and we'll work it out, don't worry."

Peter and Bernice were surprised when Simon told them that he was going to the youth club on the Friday evening, and Bernice looked concerned as well as baffled.

"Watch yourself!" She kissed Simon on the top of his head, which she never did. He presumed that she was worried about Gary and his feral gang.

Jacob had put all the lights on in the church building and the white neon light cast an unflattering, ghoulish glow on his pale face. Simon winced, imagining himself to look equally as unattractive.

"Can't we turn the lights down, Jacob? This is painful!"

"But these are the only lights we have!"

"What about candles? This is a church, you must have candles!"

Jacob hesitated. "I don't know, Simon, I don't think my dad would be OK with the candles being…"

"Your dad is not here! Is he likely to pop in do you think?"

"No, he wants me to shoulder the responsibility." Responded Jacob miserably.

Simon imagined Robert saying exactly that in his cold, dour tone and felt a sharp pang of renewed pity for Jacob.

"I tell you what mate, we'll leave these hideous lights on while we prep the food, OK?"

Jacob nodded and the two of them traipsed into the dank-smelling kitchen to distribute the paltry, unappetising supplies onto paper plates. The cheap crisps, the custard creams, the cut-price orange squash was diluted in a large plastic jug.

Simon tried not to breath in the kitchen, it smelt awful. He was thinking that the candles would also help override the stench of damp.

"Why don't we just leave the snacks in here, and then people can help themselves?" Suggested Simon, thinking that people would have to be desperate to find these offerings appealing.

"Perhaps the ghost will eat them." Said Jacob, chuckling feebly.

68

Emily brought along three girls who Simon recognised from school. The four of them were the first to arrive, just after seven, the official start time. Simon had persuaded Jacob to kill the neon lights and the grim institutional space was much improved by the manic flickering of multiple large white candles which were attached to the walls.

"These are only supposed to be lit for important ceremonies, Simon!" Jacob was still concerned, as he took them carefully out of a cupboard in the kitchen.

"This is an important occasion, Jacob! Live a little!" By then, all that Simon was thinking about was seeing Emily again and hopefully getting an opportunity to kiss her.

Despite his bad memories of the school in Tensit, it was somehow pleasant to see those girls again. Simon was a sociable boy at heart and without realising it, he had obviously missed the lack of social interaction that had become his norm during the last weeks. Also, wearing ordinary clothes, they all looked almost completely different. Simon's brain somehow barely associated those girls with school in those clothes and in that light. Also, they came across, at that moment, as extremely friendly and concerned.

Two of them had plastic bags in their hands, the contents of which were making a suspicious clinking noise. They were standing there sheepishly, clearly unsure whether alcohol would be allowed.

Of course, it wouldn't be allowed and Simon didn't think that Jacob would overlook this breach of protocol.

At that point, Jacob was just standing there, uncertainly, in the space in front of the altar. Besides him, on a plastic chair, were a pile of board games. The expression on his face was somehow both worried and gormless.

Simon somehow managed to usher Jacob into the kitchen, under the guise of bringing out some crisps. He hoped that the girls would be canny enough to disguise the alcohol effectively in the meantime. He was relieved to note, in fact, that when he and Jacob emerged from the kitchen, the girls were standing around looking demure and unassuming and apparently holding plastic glasses of orange juice.

"Oh, you already have drinks! That's good!" Proclaimed Jacob innocently. "We have more squash in the kitchen if you want!"

The girls tittered and giggled. They looked much prettier and older in the candle light with their jeans and fitted tops and make up. To please Jacob, more than anything, Simon organised a 'Connect 4' tournament and surprisingly, they got quite into it. They had hidden the vodka bottle in one of their bags and every time Jacob went into the kitchen, which fortunately he did a lot as he took his responsibility as host seriously, they would top themselves up.

By the time the group of boys showed up, the girls were all drunk and Emily and Simon had been flirting seriously for at least half an hour.

Simon felt himself stiffen when the four boys walked in. They weren't the boys that were normally associated with Gary and his gang, but nevertheless, they hadn't been friendly to him in school either, nor had they defended him from his bullies. They had cans of beer with them and made no pretence at hiding them.

They scoffed openly at the sight of the Connect 4 and Simon could immediately feel the weight of Jacob's worried gaze as he tried to catch Simon's eye.

69

Simon sighed heavily. Literally all he wanted to do was flirt with Emily, but he was smart enough to realise that if these boys were allowed to run riot, there would be no more Friday youth club, and no more opportunity for the flirting.

"Look!" He stood up and addressed them immediately before he lost his nerve, making sure to stand as straight as possible.

"This is our only opportunity to have fun in Constance, for you guys too! We can enjoy ourselves but if we don't listen to Jacob here, the social club won't be able to continue."

The boys looked sceptically from Simon to Jacob (who was staring at the ground), and back again. One of them started chuckling.

"Are you like his…boyfriend?"

The other boys all tittered and guffawed and Simon sensed Jacob beside him, blush a deep obvious pink, clearly visible even by candlelight. Simon, was, for a moment, struck dumb. Just as he was formulating a response however, Emily spoke up. She stood up straight as she spoke. Slight as she was, she still somehow managed to be imposing.

"Are you really as dumb as you look, collectively, I mean? Actually, don't even bother answering that, I know you are! I have known all of you forever. Do you not realise that this is the only opportunity that any of us have, in this crappy village, for hanging out with each other, unsupervised and pretty much free to do what we want?" At that point, she let her gaze fall meaningfully on the plastic glass she was holding in her hand.

"All we have to do is agree not to take the piss and not to be obvious (another meaningful glance) and then we will be as free as it is possible for any of us to be here!"

The boys shuffled uncomfortably and surreptitiously glanced at the one who was known to be the most outspoken there, James, their unofficial spokesperson.

Simon was thinking how attractive Emily looked when she was all fired up, but at the same time, he partially resented how she was always having to stand up and speak for him, and how they seemed to listen to her more than to him.

"OK" James finally muttered. "But do we really have to play Connect 4?"

"No!" Jacob interjected brightly, "I also have Monopoly, Cluedo, and Mousetrap!"

Everyone laughed and just like that the tension dissipated. Emily and Simon exchanged loaded glances. The boys hid their beers and the girls hid their vodka, but everyone still got drunk and the atmosphere remained good natured. Simon could never work out, not that night nor during the subsequent Friday night sessions, whether Jacob really couldn't see what was going on or just pretended not to. Once he made a cryptic comment to Simon about smoke and mirrors, which made Simon think that Jacob was already very used to pretence, that he was smarter than he seemed, that maybe he knew very well that he was being played.

Simon and Emily were not the only teenage couple at the youth club. Inevitably, many of the others paired up too, and an unofficial routine developed whereby the young couples would take it in turns to sneak off during the playing of the board games to go and kiss each other in the graveyard.

Jacob absolutely must have noticed the couples sneaking out, there were never more than twelve kids there and it was totally obvious, but again, he did not say anything. Simon, would glance over at Jacob sometimes, when he was in the middle of playing a game, and there would be a big relaxed grin on his face. It would be at times like that when Simon would realise that these evenings were a type of escape for Jacob too.

Things carried on in this vein and pleasant times were had by all until Christmas, when the whole thing imploded.

70

Both of Simon's parents seemed too miserable and distracted to worry about him missing school. As the weeks went by and Simon fully recovered from the attack in the wood, he himself grew concerned. It was his GCSE year, he had been absent three weeks by then, obviously he was missing important chunks of information in all his subjects. He was amazed that his parents had not come to the same conclusion themselves and acted upon it, and yet it was like this dark impenetrable cloud had descended upon the pair of them.

Both Bernice and Peter seemed depressed and yet they did not seem, in Simon's perplexed view, united in their misery; the seemed sad and distracted for different reasons which confused Simon all the more.

Simon himself was feeling far stronger and more cheerful as the village trudged towards Winter, mainly because of his relationship with Emily which was enjoying that ecstatic golden phase of young love. Because of the strictness of her parents, the couple only got to see each other on the Friday night at the youth club, but they spoke to each other every day on the phone. The illicit nature of their relationship furthermore added a frisson to the proceedings. Who knows whether it wouldn't all have fizzled out quicker had they been allowed to see each other whenever they wanted?

Simon finally persuaded his mother to address the issue of his education.

"Yes, yes, you're right of course!" Bernice admitted, seeming both frazzled and guilty that she had neglected him. "I can't imagine that you want to return to that school though, I don't know…"

In Bernice's head, was the idea that they were on the point of leaving that awful place, that they would be returning to London shortly, but she couldn't tell Simon that until it was definite.

"I phoned the council in Cavershall and told them about the issue, explained it all."

"You called the council? In Cavershall?" Bernice was simultaneously proud of Simon's resourcefulness and yet still somehow panicky.

"I explained," Simon continued "about the bullying in that school and the attack by Gary and how it wasn't possible for me to return there and stay safe, and as there are no other options close to Constance, the woman I spoke to suggested a home-schooling program."

"But Simon! I can't teach you!" Cried Bernice, fully panicked then. Of course, she would have been able to teach him under normal circumstances, but her head was not in a good space.

"No, no, it's OK!" Simon was bewildered by his mother's passionate reaction. "There are books they send you, and any subject that you find difficult, they send you a tutor. Apparently, it's an initiative they often use in these rural places, because loads of kids drop out of formal education."

"Right." Bernice nodded, still thinking to herself that the Jensons would be out of Constance after Christmas anyway, so it didn't matter what she agreed to.

Simon himself, therefore, organised his home school program, and a bunch of study guides arrived for all his subjects promptly. He himself determined that he could cope with all of them himself, except for science. Further communication with the council resulted, therefore, in a bespectacled older lady in a tattered mini, driving over to the cottage in Constance on a Tuesday and Thursday, in order to teach Simon Combined Science.

71

Bernice, at that point, was still seeing Alex every week or so. She no longer made-up excuses when she asked for the car, although neither did she explain what she needed it for. They would always meet in the incongruously cool café in Cavershall and then go back to his hotel room. He had quickly relinquished the charm offensive and was once again indifferent with bouts of cruelty. He blamed Bernice for the inconvenience of her stay in Constance, for how disruptive it was to his own life to have to leave London and take a hotel in Cavershall just so that he could see her, how expensive it was. When he was feeling particularly nasty, he told her that she wasn't even worth it.

Bernice wished she had the strength of character to tell him not to come anymore, to tell him that she didn't even want to see him anymore. The words were always on the tip of her tongue, yet somehow, they remained there and she never managed to speak. She felt as if she was collapsing inside like a deck of cards. She didn't have the energy to fight back or even react against anything, that was how she felt.

Sarah had started asking her for money. It was blackmail in exchange for Sarah not using her contacts to get Peter sacked from the factory, or not telling Peter that Bernice was having an affair; it was one or the other or both. The threats seemed interchangeable, but both, in Bernice's befuddled panicked mind, seemed valid.

It was a relief, almost, when Sarah finally asked for money. Aha! thought Bernice, almost with triumph; I knew she wanted something and finally, here it is. It was common and garden in the end, just money like any other blackmailer. Bernice had nothing but contempt for Sarah, but she was still afraid of her and she still paid her.

"This would never have happened," Sarah dared suggest once, at their meeting place in a nearby field, "If your snotty family had tithed the church like everyone else does."

Bernice didn't bother to reply. She used the money that Peter gave her for household expenses to pay Sarah, which meant that the family's diet changed suddenly and drastically. Suddenly, almost overnight, they all became vegetarian and their meals consisted mainly of potatoes and rice.

Peter didn't even seem to notice but Simon did. When he questioned his mother, however, she mumbled something about vegetables being healthier and refused to engage further. He himself would try to fill up on the cheap white bread that suddenly appeared in the kitchen. It tasted of cardboard and the only thing that made it remotely palatable was the cheap margarine which fortunately also appeared.

December dawned in the village. It was Advent.

The family did not go to mass. Simon was far happier than he had been but both Peter and Bernice were unravelling. Poppy was due back home for her Christmas break and the anticipation of that sustained Bernice in particular. She felt as if she was imprisoned in Constance with Sarah as the evil jailer and Poppy would be a visitor from the free world. At times, Bernice tried to talk to Peter, but he seemed both physically unwell and mentally detached. In the Winter fog which seeped in at the kitchen window, he looked prematurely old and haggard and it was hard to reconcile the stooped, defeated individual he had become with the energetic, optimistic man who had arrived to manage the factory back in August.

Constance had poisoned them, thought Bernice. There was no other way to describe it.

72

"It was Victor who was stalking me, well, following me anyway, that is who I think you saw." Poppy told her friends.

"Victor?" Tina frowned.

"Yeah, remember I told you about him? The boy in the youth hostel I hung out with briefly in the summer?"

"I remember!" Declared one of the boys, lighting a cigarette theatrically, as he always did. "Goth boy!"

"Yup, well done for paying attention!"

"No, no" Said the other boy frowning, "It is definitely a girl whom I saw, I can tell the difference you know!"

"Well, very likely Linda hanging out where you saw her had nothing to do with me, as I said before…"

"OK, OK, if you say so!"

Poppy felt unaccountably cross. She was a bit tired of the constant drama around her new friends. She was feeling rundown in general and looking forward to seeing her family over the Christmas break. Simon's calls had been far more cheerful of late, and reading between the lines, she realised that he had a girlfriend and she was happy for him. Somehow, from a distant she missed him more and was far less inclined to indulge in the sibling teasing and rivalry which would always go on when the two of them were together.

Poppy's mother, however, sounded increasingly weird on the phone and Poppy was disconcerted by that. She sounded depressed and vague, almost as if she was drugged, although Poppy knew that could not possibly be the case. Her father, on the other hand, the few times she had spoken to him, sounded exhausted.

Poppy was eager to see the two of them. She wasn't sure why or how they had deteriorated since arriving in Constance, yet apparently, they had. There was only a week or so left of the university term before they all broke up for the holidays and parties and festivities abounded everywhere. The whole of Nottingham seemed a hive of frenzied Christmas-related activity.

It was outside the toilets of a club that Poppy next saw Linda. Poppy was quite drunk as she stumbled out of the toilet into the dimly-lit corridor outside it. Linda seemed to appear suddenly. Poppy looked up and she was just standing there with her long hair and flowing hippy skirts suddenly appearing dated and much older than the rest of the cohort. In that club, the girls were all wearing jeans and crop tops, hip hop was playing.

The corridor was quite narrow and Linda blocked Poppy's way. Beneath the fuzziness of the alcohol, Poppy felt a low-lying panic.

"You have ruined my life!" Linda hissed angrily and Poppy attempted to snort in derision, but she was anxious.

"Don't be ridiculous!" She retaliated, but her voice was shaky and no match for the boom of the bass. "This is all so silly! I just made a group of friends, like normal people do at university, you didn't have to become all weird about it!"

It was so loud in there, that Poppy realised that Linda could not hear her, and would probably not listen even if she could. She herself watched Linda's mouth, she was screeching something about how she had thought they were best friends, how Poppy had betrayed her. As she shrieked her face was right up close to Poppy's and her breath smelt sour. Poppy was overcome by revulsion and yet she was too inebriated to scrape together the necessary energy to push past Linda and run.

The whole situation would have continued indefinitely, had not a gaggle of girls arrived to queue for the toilet. Poppy used the distraction to push past them as they filed past, and disappear into the club to cleave to her friends.

73

There were a few uninspiring and cheap Christmas decorations listlessly draped from the lampposts in Constance. Gaudy gold-coloured giant plastic stars which had seen better days and were worn away in places.

The shop which sold everything had a couple of the same shabby stars hanging from its awning outside, all the establishments in the village did; it was clearly a common theme and a traditional decoration which got dragged out every year. Inside the shop, however, someone had gone mad draping multicoloured strands of tinsel over every available surface, over all the produce too, so that if you wanted to buy anything at all, you would have to carefully lift the tinsel from it first. Bernice, standing by the till and waiting to pay wondered if a child had done it. The couple who owned the shop were as cold-eyed and dry as everyone else in Constance, it seemed far-fetched to presume that they were responsible for the manic tinsel scattering.

A bit later that day, Bernice went to meet Alex in their usual café. Despite everything, Bernice appreciated the effort that the town of Cavershall had made with the decorations, they were far superior to those of Constance, on another level entirely. Multicoloured fairy lights zig-zagged across the high street and formed the shape of Christmas Trees on the lampposts. In their café, candle light provided a cosiness to detract from the dreary afternoon outside and in the corner a real Christmas tree, decorated tastefully, emitted an intoxicating smell of pine needles.

Bernice was in quite a good mood that day, all things considered, and the prettiness of the café had perked her up further. One look at Alex's dour face, however, and she could have accurately predicted that it wasn't going to last.

He waited until the waitress had taken their order, all the while keeping his gaze fixated on Bernice's face. This was weird behaviour even from him and Bernice felt disconcerted.

"What is it?" She exclaimed, as soon as the waitress had gone.

"I have something to tell you." Alex's eyes still glared at her intensely.

"You're married!" Joked Bernice nervously. It wasn't really a joke, and she wasn't smiling.

"No, nothing like that. I want to tell you the reason I picked you."

"Picked me?" Confusion came to Bernice first, "What do you mean 'picked me,' your dog ran into me in the park!"

"Yeah." Short unpleasant bark of a laugh. "That was staged."

"Staged? It wasn't a coincidental meeting?" Bernice started feeling anxious. There was something off about Alex, she could see it clearly now. The wound up intensity, the way he switched moods, went from charming to furious and disdainful in seconds. He wasn't furious then, he was just staring at her hard, in a creepy way, wanting to shock her obviously, and she was, of course, shocked.

"But why then? What did you want from me?"

"I wanted what I got!" He snorted with mirthless laughter.

"But why me then? What did I do to deserve…"

"'Deserve,' Is it? Haven't you had a good time with me?"

Bernice didn't reply. It was very warm in the café but she felt a cold chill run through her. The smiling waitress approached carrying two steaming mugs of coffee and Alex rewarded her with his warm smile. Bernice was shocked anew at how he could turn the warmth off and on.

"I went to school with Peter," he stated calmly when the waitress had left. "He was mean to me, bullied me, although I dislike that word. I wanted revenge, all my life I wanted revenge, and that is what you are for, a means to an end." The harsh bark of laughter again.

Bernice's logical mind immediately started calculating. Was that even possible? Did their ages tally? Obviously, Alex had lied about where he had grown up, but the dates, the ages, yes it was feasible…

"Cat got your tongue? Aren't you going to tell me that it's not possible?"

Bernice was gaping at him and she didn't even realise. She was trying to remember anything that Peter had said about his childhood or his time at school, but any conversations they had had about their young lives were themselves so long ago. Peter went to an ordinary high school, obviously he was clever, Bernice had no recollection of any additional information having ever been presented to her, either by Peter or his family, not when they first met and not subsequently.

"What exactly did Peter do to you?" She asked finally. The café had started playing a compilation of Christmas songs. Jingle Bells had just begun, the sound of jolly bells filled the café.

Alex explained that Peter had beaten him up on a regular basis and broken his ribs on more than one occasion. But he had already lied to Bernice so much, that she could not be sure whether he was lying then, and she was determined, somehow, out of self-preservation, not to believe him.

Looking at Peter's haggard, tired face later, it was hard to reconcile all that Alec had accused him of, and Bernice put it all firmly to the back of her mind.

74

The entrance of the factory was bedecked with shiny strands of holly and in the corner of the reception area, an enormous white plastic tree was covered in red baubles and multi-coloured lights. Cardboard boxes were arranged underneath, wrapped in paper and ribbon as if to imitate real presents.

Peter, lost in his own thoughts, barely saw any of it. Bernice had taken the car that day again and he had caught the bus to work. He didn't feel any better, the exhaustion was not lifting and quite often he felt a dull weight in his chest, which he attributed still to stress. He did his job on autopilot but far too slowly and with an utter lack of interest or enthusiasm, and it was becoming increasingly clear to him that things were coming to a head. In fact, that was what Peter was thinking about right then, that morning, that he would have to stop working there, imminently, or as soon as possible.

Having arrived at this conclusion, he felt a warm relief flood through him and even managed to smile cheerfully at June. He had decided, it was fixed. He would hand in his notice later that day which would mean that his last working day would be New Years Eve and then they could all get the hell out of that awful village and move back to London.

They could all make a fresh start in the new year. The finances? Well, they would just have to work that out later. It wasn't worth it, it wasn't worth living like this just to stay above the breadline. Even being dirt poor in London, they would have to be happier than this. God knows, they couldn't possibly be any less happy than they were now.

At the Friday youth club, Simon noted that someone, Sarah probably, had made a decent, albeit slightly tacky, attempt to decorate the church. There were lots of tiny plastic trees in various garish colours tacked up onto the walls. All of them had red baubles on them, they must have come like that, Simon thought; some cheap factory job lot.

It all seemed quite gaudy and incongruous and not in keeping with the dour grey atmosphere within the hall, but then perhaps Sarah had been imbued with a flash of Christmas spirit! Cheerful and in love, Simon was in the mood to think the best of people.

Just beneath the altar, occupying much of the space where the kids played or pretended to play board games on Friday evenings, there was a much more traditional nativity scene, with large, badly painted plaster cast figures staged around baby Jesus, a doll, in a manger filled with an abundance of real straw. There was Joseph and Mary, three kings, a couple of shepherds, an angel suspended perilously from the roof of the manger, and an assortment of farm animals including a disproportionately large hare, which made all the kids giggle.

Despite their alcohol and their cynicism, the kids who met there for the Friday night youth club were fond of the decorations and in particular, of the nativity scene. It brought to mind more innocent times perhaps, a nostalgia for a simpler childish perspective, a naivety since lost.

The routine at the youth club never varied, the kids never pushed their luck again by drinking or snogging in sight of Jacob, and it was never really clear what Jacob noticed or understood. The atmosphere was jolly and relaxed, and Simon had observed that Jacob smiled and laughed a lot too; he obviously really loved playing the board games, which the others mostly only pretended to be interested in. His entire focus, on those Friday nights, would be on whichever game they were playing, and he didn't see, or at least he didn't seem to notice the kids sneak in and out.

75

The journey from Nottingham to Constance was complicated and arduous involving many forms of transport, and, when Poppy finally arrived, on the bus from Tensit, she felt as if she had been travelling for days.

Because both her parents had sounded so stressed on the phone, she had not wanted to bother them by asking to be picked up from the train station in Cavershall, which would, in fact, have made things a lot easier. She didn't even tell them what time she was arriving. It was 7pm on a Thursday, and a freezing sleet was falling. It was so much colder in Constance than it was in Nottingham and Poppy drew her thick padded jacket tightly around her. She had never been to the cottage, although she had at some point seen a photograph, probably in London before they had moved there when everyone was all excited about Peter's new job.

The vague memory of the photograph was useless now in the dark. She took the piece of paper with the address scrawled on it out of her coat pocket and squinted at it under the light of a lamppost from which a gaudy gold star was hanging. She was greatly relieved to discover that the cottage was quite close, but was horrified at the sight of her father who responded to her enthusiastic knocking on the door.

Peter, to Poppy's eyes, looked so much older and greyer. The process of aging had accelerated on him somehow as if he had, in Constance, entered a different time zone. It was very shocking and for long seconds, Poppy struggled to speak; she hugged him instead. She felt the hard jutting bones of his spine beneath her fingers; who was this elderly man?

"Come through, come through!" He cried, "Your mother is in the kitchen!" Peter seemed ecstatic that Poppy was there and she felt immediately guilty that she hadn't visited sooner.

Her mother didn't look much better, her face looked drawn and haggard in the harsh unrelenting light, and Poppy was shocked as well by the stiff, uncomfortable space that they were living in. At university, Poppy had missed the cosiness of their house in London, the soft furnishings and dim, homely lighting. Clearly none of that had been replicated here.

Her parents were both dressed differently too, in beige, shapeless garments. The dull clothing looked startling on both of them, but on her mother it looked particularly shocking. Poppy recalled Bernice dressing up in London, looking smart. Now she had let her hair grow out so that a thick line of dense grey was visible at the roots and obviously she was not wearing make-up. Her skin in the unflattering glare, seemed papery and lined.

"This place is…different…" Poppy swallowed. She had been shown the kitchen and the living room, there was nothing else to see downstairs. A candle was flickering on the dining table to disguise the damp smell, but it was still discernible. A small, optimistic, Christmas tree sat in the corner. The fairy lights were the same ones that Poppy remembered from childhood and she felt a sharp pang of nostalgia.

She heard pounding on the stairs and there was her brother. At least Simon looked exactly as Poppy remembered him, just a bit taller maybe. That was a huge relief. He seemed bouncy and happy and Poppy was tempted to start teasing him about his girlfriend and young love, but she felt oddly shy. It felt like a very long time since she had last seen any of them, the strangeness of the place seemed to exacerbate this. It almost felt as if they would have to get to know each other all over again.

76

During the next days, Poppy was shown around the village, although there was little to see of course, and even with the cheap Christmas decorations, she was shocked at how bleak it was.

Bernice was eager to tell her that her father had handed in his notice at the factory, and in the new year they would be moving back to London.

"It's a shame it didn't work out." Mused Bernice, "We gave it a go, but it's just…not a particularly nice place." She chuckled drily. "That's an understatement, actually, it's a shit hole and we've all had a hell of a time of it!"

Poppy was a bit shocked. Her mother had never spoken to her so bluntly before. She seemed disturbed in a way, haunted by something.

"Life is a series of…papercuts…and some people can brush them off, some people barely notice them, but some of them are deeper than others and then…"

Poppy raised her eyebrows. She had no idea what her mother was talking about. They were both wearing wellington boots and had been trudging through the muddy, freezing fields. Back at the tiny row of shops, Poppy turned to gaze at the ugly concrete hall.

"What is that?"

Bernice snorted. "That is their church."

Poppy had been told that it was unfriendly, but that Simon went there to a youth club and that was where he saw his girlfriend. That was all she knew. She understood that Simon no longer went to school, which surprised her. He had always been such a sociable boy, capable of getting on with everyone.

As they were standing there, a large woman wearing a tent-like, sagging coat approached them. Next to her, Poppy felt Bernice stiffen and her breath quicken.

The woman grinned, revealing terrible teeth.

"This must be your daughter, she's the spit of you…although, here we are not used to teenagers dying their hair." Poppy's hair had been growing out but was still bleached blonde at the ends. She stared at the woman taken-aback, what a weird, over-familiar thing to say.

"Well, we are not from here, we are from London." Poppy retorted immediately, her own voice clear in the freezing air, and the woman lost her grin and regarded her coolly.

"Yes, you certainly are." She stated in a sarcastic bark, and walked off.

"Wow!" Poppy turned to her mother as they watched Sarah off down the rain drenched street. "Who the hell was that?"

Bernice gave a wry smile and explained most of it but not all, not the blackmail.

"I wish I had stood up to her a long time ago like you did just then." She told Poppy. "It would have saved me a lot of anxiety."

"You were stuck here, I guess," Poppy shrugged, "You had no choice but try to get on with people."

It was strange for Poppy to see her mother so vulnerable. Living in the village, amongst these people seemed to have weakened her somewhat, made her insecure and anxious. Poppy told Bernice this. For the first time, their relationship seemed to have become that of equals. If anything, it was Poppy who sometimes felt like the adult. She felt, oddly, as if she had come to Constance in order to save her family who were floundering, even drowning. Her parents certainly seemed to be in a weirdly dark place.

Bernice didn't tell Poppy about Alex, but she did tell her about other problems that had pre-dated their sojourn in the village. She hinted heavily that things between her and Peter had not been great for many years. She felt bad spelling that out for Poppy, he was her dad after all. Poppy wasn't an idiot though, she had spent years wondering if her parents would get divorced. It was obvious that the vibe hadn't been warm between them for ages.

77

Weirdly, knowing that this was the last few weeks that the Jensons would have to ever spend in Constance, imbued that Christmas holiday period with a great sense of celebration, with a hint of rebellious recklessness. They treated that period, collectively, as a holiday in an unpleasant place that they were obliged to make the most of.

A letter arrived at the cottage from the University accommodation office, saying that a room was available for Poppy in the same halls of residence as Tina and the boys. She would be staying on a different floor, but that didn't matter. The way Poppy saw it was that she would finally be free of Linda and the bedsit and she was ecstatic.

Peter was still working his notice period and Simon studied a great deal at home. Even though schools were officially on holiday for Christmas, he still worked hard, particularly in the subjects he was weaker in. The idea of returning to London had encouraged him to get ahead. He didn't want to find himself to have fallen far behind his classmates when he returned. Poppy once asked him how he felt about leaving his girlfriend and his face fell a bit, but then he shrugged.

"If it is meant to be we will find each other again." Simon replied philosophically.

Poppy somehow doubted that Emily saw things like that. She wondered if Simon had even told her that he was leaving, but she did not ask him. He was old enough now to manage his own relationships and to make his own mistakes.

Poppy and Bernice spent their time going for walks through endless fields and woods when it wasn't raining, bundled up against the ubiquitous freezing wind. They deliberately avoided the row of shops, but when they did chance to bump into anyone, anywhere, any of the villagers, they ignored them. Bernice no longer felt as if she needed to make an effort. It was a huge relief, and she felt as if all the tension had somehow melted away. She stopped paying Sarah, because Peter was leaving the factory anyway. The worst Sarah could do was tell Peter about her affair with Alex and there was no proof, just her word. There was nothing Bernice could do about that possibility and she made the tough decision to risk it. She no longer wanted that dreadful woman to have any power over her. Maybe Poppy's return had emboldened her too; she no longer felt so alone and somehow powerless.

By the same token, Bernice no longer met up with Alex either. Now that she knew it was all part of some strange revenge on Peter, that the whole thing was artificially manufactured, there really was no point in continuing their sordid little affair, especially as it really didn't make her happy. Had it ever made her happy? She really wasn't sure.

And if it hadn't made her happy then what on earth had been the point of it? She felt, suddenly and inexplicably, more relaxed and content than she had done since they had arrived in Constance and maybe even happier than she had felt before that, still in London, whilst under the spell of Alex. The presence of a clear-eyed, more mature Poppy somehow imbued her with a spirit of recklessness and rebellion. Both Sarah and Alex kept phoning so Bernice unplugged the landline.

Once, Sarah came to the front door too. Bernice could see her bloated silhouette through the mottled glass. At that point, even though the radio was blaring and someone was obviously in, Bernice and Poppy hid in the kitchen like giggling kids until she went away. Bernice had not told Poppy the reason why she was avoiding Sarah, the whole thing felt sordid and shameful to her.

A few days before Christmas, Bernice and Poppy took the car and drove to a huge brand-new supermarket complex near Cavershall to buy supplies. The shopping centre had been professionally decorated and the air was fragrant with the sugary sweet aroma of the mince pies and the cakes on sale everywhere. Christmas carols played loudly and Bernice brushed aside her tarnished memories of them as background music as Alex spouted forth his toxic motivation for their affair.

Poppy and Bernice linked arms and went shopping as if neither of them had a care in the world.

78

Simon and Emily, during the school term, had only seen each other at the youth club on Friday nights. Now, during the school holidays, and that things between them had become both more serious and more physical, they were both desperate to meet more often.

Simon could have invited Emily to his house, but, recognising that his parents were already in a fragile condition, he did not want to draw further negative attention to them or potentially attract the ire of Emily's family and bring that to their door. Instead, Emily pretended she was meeting a female friend and the two would bundle up against the bitter cold and meet in the frozen silence of the winter woodland.

Simon sometimes had unpleasant flashbacks of the attack by Gary and his gang, and his head would whip round at the tiny sound of every snapping twig, but it was far too brutally cold in the woods for the likes of Gary and his sycophants to venture out of their warm homes and nature kept their assignations secret.

Peter had told his family on the very day that he had handed in his resignation at the factory, so that Simon was completely aware that the Jensons were packing up and leaving on the 1st of January. He did not tell Emily. He somehow thought that she might have found out from a different source about his father resigning from the factory, the village being what it was, but she had not, at least not yet.

Simon felt a bit bad about that, he knew it was cowardly of him, yet he rationalised it by telling himself that what Emily didn't know wouldn't hurt her. He had instructed Bernice to purchase Emily an elaborate gift on her excursion to the fancy shopping centre. He was thinking that it would be both a Christmas present and an apologetic goodbye.

On Christmas day, the Jensons adhered to the same well-worn traditions that they had always practised in London too. Bernice always placed the kids' stockings at the bottom of their beds, old red wool stockings, bought when they were infants and now falling apart at the seams but imbued with years of memories. Breakfast was always eggs with smoked salmon and 'fizzy wine' for the adults. Then everyone would open presents from each other under the tree. In the years since Poppy and Simon had hit adolescence, the pretence of Father Christmas had been logically abandoned.

That year, painfully aware of their perilous financial situation, the presents were meagre, merely symbolic. There was lots of chocolate and warm socks and thick jumpers. Everyone was on board with that though and Poppy and Simon were old enough to completely understand.

In London, the Jensons would have gone to church, but here in Constance, they had no intention at all of subjecting themselves to the frigid atmosphere in the hall, so they had stayed at home and played board games until lunch and then bundled up against the cold to go for a brisk walk in the surrounding fields. A pale sun was peaking weakly from behind greyish clouds and inevitably, the family passed familiar faces from the village, some they nodded to. From a distance, Simon glimpsed Gary and his family, all in their bizarre old-fashioned garb, and he shuddered within. Simon had not seen Gary at all since the attack in the woods. Every Friday, at the youth club, he would worry that he would suddenly appear, he never stopped being on edge every time the door opened, and yet somehow, for whatever reason, Gary stayed away.

Jacob, at their last meeting had encouraged everyone there to attend church on Christmas Day. His grey eyes had rested heavily on Simon as he said it. Simon didn't blame Jacob; it was a script he was obliged to repeat. Jacob himself was a weak vessel, easily manipulated but fundamentally kindly. It was obviously for Simon's benefit though as the others, all from Constance, would never dream of not attending church. Their parents all tithed, they had probably never even questioned the logic of it. The way they saw it, their entire lives on earth and after were tied to Richard and The Church of the Divine.

The next youth club happened to fall on New Years Eve and a celebration was planned. Not a party in the traditional sense, but a celebration with a quiz and better, more exciting, food and drink. Even Jacob had acknowledged that their usual offerings were miserable, and mainly ended up uneaten and in the bin.

New Years Eve was also the next time that Simon would see Emily, as she was going away to visit relatives with her family between Christmas and the New Year. Simon had yet to give her the present and he was excited for that.

The day of New Years Eve dawned sunny and bright and frost everywhere reflected brilliant glimmers of light. It was Friday, a work day, Peter's last day at the factory and he drove in that morning with a wide smile on his face, the first time he had ever done so.

79

The factory floor was still busy, the workers there rotated in shifts and the machines never stopped. However, the management floor was quiet, it had been all week, as many of the office workers took annual leave between Christmas and New Year.

June was there that day, serious and industrious. She had only taken one extra day off. That was the kind of person she was, a person who preferred to think of herself as useful, a person for whom relaxation was not particularly pleasant and felt, more than anything, like a waste of time.

Peter did not have that much to do that day, beyond leave everything tidy, administration wise, for his successor. He had been told that someone would take over from him, but he did not know who it was.

Bernice and Poppy were relaxing in the living room watching Christmas films, when Simon departed to go to the youth club just after 5pm, Emily's present under his arm. The 'party' was scheduled to start a bit earlier, at five. It was already pitch dark in the village by then, except for the streetlights. The tattered remains of the Christmas stars hung sadly from the lamp posts, some fairy lights still twinkled gamely from dying trees in some houses. Simon felt buoyant and happy right up until the moment he walked into the church and saw Robert in the place where Jacob always sat at the front with his board games.

For some reason, panic twisted in Simon's gut and the door slamming behind him caused him to jump. Robert was sitting next to a cheap foldout table in front of the alter which was laden with party food. He was wearing fashionable jeans and a shirt, an outfit which looked odd on him, all wrong. He seemed like a grizzled actor playing the role of a much younger man. Sitting around him, in their usual spots, were the other kids who usually attended the youth club, including Emily (who smiled widely at Simon). Some of the teens seemed apprehensive, but none of them appeared actually fearful, which reassured Simon a tiny bit. After all, these kids had known Robert their entire lives.

"Ah, Simon!" Robert intoned, "How good of you to join us! I am afraid Jacob couldn't attend this evening as he has a bad cold, but still, as you know, we have a special little celebration tonight and as, Jacob tells me, you kids are always in charge..." He chuckled darkly, "I have even organised the lighting to your specifications."

The whole speech seemed to be directed at Simon which was disconcerting. It was true, he noted, the candles had been lit along the walls as they always were on Friday evenings. Only now, their flickering lights were reflected in the cheap plastic trees which were affixed near them.

"Sarah," Robert went on, "Has also prepared a special Christmas drink which we always enjoy at home during this period, and insisted I bring it for all of you to try!"

Three large old-fashioned glass bottles full of some purple liquid were sitting on the table, and Simon could see that the other kids were already drinking it.

"It's tasty!" Chirped one of the boys, "Tastes like a kind of thick sweet blackcurrant squash!"

"Tuck in!" Insisted Robert gaily, "All of you! And then we'll play some games and do a fun Christmas quiz!"

80

Peter was having a little snooze at his desk after the carb-heavy lunch he had ingested in the canteen. It being Christmas, for weeks now, the menu had featured roast meats of various kinds, potatoes and all the traditional trimmings, as well as particularly tasty giant mince pies. As it was all free for everyone who worked there, it was hard to resist.

He had been thinking, during the entire Christmas period, and the thought came to Peter again then, that he and Bernice were in a much better, more solid place than they had been for many years. They were good friends now rather than jealous lovers, that was what Peter thought. The important thing, the most important thing was that their kids were happy and settled and they seemed to have succeeded in that, or at least they were on their way to succeeding with Simon. There was a great deal to be said, mused Peter to himself, lulled into a half-dream there at his desk, a great deal to be said for a simple and enduring friendship.

When Dennis suddenly appeared before him, his trademark smirk smeared wide across his face, Peter first thought that he had dozed off and was having a nightmare. He felt his skin immediately grow clammy with sweat and he shook his head violently in order to wake up. Dennis was not supposed to be there, June would not have let him past without warning Peter beforehand.

"Your new elderly guard dog was not on her perch." Said Dennis, and it was at that moment that Peter realised that he was, in fact, unfortunately awake.

"I guess they didn't tell you that I'll be taking over from you." Dennis carried on with his repellent little voice and Peter did not trust himself to speak. The urge to punch Dennis's slimy face was huge within him, and he needed all his strength and self-control to resist.

"You're taking over from me?" Peter could hear his own voice but it seemed to float over to him from some distance away. He did not feel well.

Back at the church, Robert had insisted that the kids carry on as normal, just as they would have done had Jacob been at the helm, but they couldn't do that of course. There was no sneaking out with Robert there. They just sat around and ate and drank and played board games. The purple drink was very tasty and addictive somehow, and Simon felt, (they all felt), that the more they drank of it, the happier and more relaxed they felt.

Robert sat is his chair and watched them play the various wholesome boardgames on a tatty rug on the floor. He smiled indulgently like a benign uncle but he didn't play the games with them, as Jacob had always done, and it seemed to Simon, who had started to feel a bit woozy, that Robert was resting his eyes mostly on him.

At some point, as the candles flickered down onto a monopoly board, and most of the purple drink had been consumed, the kids started saying that they felt dizzy and sick. One by one, they got up and told Robert sorry, but they felt ill and could they be excused. They looked pale and sweaty and wobbly and Robert let them go. His eyes tracked them as they swayed lightly towards the exit, some clutching their stomachs.

Simon had somehow always known that there would be no quiz.

Emily left too, with the present Simon had given her clutched under one arm. Before she left, she grabbed his hand and squeezed it. There was no way of speaking without Robert hearing, his eyes were trained on them, on the couple, but mainly on Simon.

Simon felt Emily's fear though, and apprehension, he knew her well enough by then. She was not usually emotional; if she was scared, there was a good reason. He was feeling light surges of nausea by then anyway, and there were only four other kids left.

He stood up, a bit shakily from the ground where he and the others all sat, mainly cross-legged. The distance from sitting to standing seemed much longer than it should have done. Simon felt an unpleasant spinning sensation. Around him blurred the pretty flickering candlelight, the gaudy tiny baubles on the plastic trees, the childish, pallid faces of the other teens. Robert seemed much larger suddenly, solid and immovable as a truck. He was watching Simon still and then a trickle of fear came, gently at first.

"I'm going to go now." Simon said. "Thank you for the party, but I am not feeling great."

"Of course, of course!" Said Robert smoothly, "But first could you get me a glass of water from the kitchen, my knees are a bit painful today and it's hard for me to stand up. Be careful of the ghost! It likes to come out to play on New Years Eve!"

81

There was a sharp pain down Peter's arm and an unbelievably heavy weight on his chest. Peter sensed himself falling and hitting the side of his desk on the way down, heard Dennis' repellent voice shout something, and then nothing. A white fuzzy space.

In the revolting, pungent kitchen of the church, Simon was hunting around for a glass, but he felt disconnected from his body as if he was moving about in a dream. Everything felt weirdly complicated and then, like a pistol shot, he heard the kitchen door slam behind him. Simon was confined in that tiny malodorous space and panic arrived.

It was just after 7pm when Bernice was finally phoned and told that Peter had suffered a suspected heart attack and had been taken to the hospital in Cavershall. It would later be discovered that Dennis had fled the scene when Peter had fallen, without alerting anyone, and that an ambulance had only been called a full twelve minutes later, when June had come back from the bathroom and found him. June, herself, would take a long time to get over the shock of the discovery of Peter lying flat out on the office carpet. She had thought he was dead.

Simon banged on the kitchen door in a mad panic. It was not a well-constructed door, if Simon had not been weakened and drugged, he could probably have broken it down. He heard heavy footsteps approach from the other side.

"Have you met the ghost yet?" Roberts dark voice penetrated the thin wood. Where were the others? Simon's thoughts scrambled about desperately. Why were they not helping him? Letting him out?

The hospital in Cavershall, or rather the kindly lady on the phone, when hearing that Bernice didn't have a car (It was in the factory parking lot), told her a taxi would be sent for her. That was the protocol in emergency cases.

"This is an emergency case then?" Bernice struggled to breathe properly as she spoke.

"Yes. Yes I'm afraid it is."

When Robert finally opened the door, Simon realised immediately that there was no one else there, and that he had known, in his petrified heart, that would be the case.

"Where are the others?" His heart was hammering loudly in his chest and he felt as if he was about to vomit. The bright light of the kitchen made Robert a shadow, a rapidly-approaching sinister shadow.

"They left," Said Robert in a new voice, creepy and crooning, "I wanted to spend some time together just me and you…tell me…did you meet the ghost?"

Bernice told a very shaken Poppy to stay home because she would have to tell Simon what was going on when he got home. The taxi sped smoothly, through the silent frozen darkness. Periodically, across the shadowed fields they drove past, fireworks whizzed in optimistic spurts and splutters.

It was New Years Eve.

"It is New Years Eve" declared Robert, apropos to nothing. He was merely a step away from Simon then. Simon was still standing, trembling, in the doorway of the kitchen. "I have always known that you city kids are more experienced in the ways of the world, more so than us innocent folk; you have the devil in you."

"What?" Simon was both terrified and bewildered, but by now he had realised all too clearly what Robert wanted from him.

Robert reached out a veiny scrawny hand towards him.

82

Poppy, pacing anxiously back and forth in the tiny, uncomfortable cottage, smelt the smoke before she saw the flames. Agitated and confused, she attributed it first to something that had been left burning in their kitchen and then immediately after to potential fireworks outside somewhere, in the fields. She stood at the window in the living room which had a partial view of the path leading to the front door of the cottage, willing both Simon to return home and her mother to call from the hospital.

It was mere minutes later that Poppy glimpsed the first leaping orange flames, stark against the black overcast sky and her heart leapt in her chest. A stranger to Constance, as she was, it was still pretty evident that the flames were coming from the centre of the village, from near to where she knew her brother to be. Torn between running out into the street to see what was happening and staying home, a desperate agitation ripped through her as she stood at that window watching flames dance higher and higher and then, with some small relief, heard the wail of the fire engines. She couldn't wait any longer then, she rushed outside. Poppy wasn't wearing a coat but the fire had heated the surrounding houses like a giant oven and even as she joined the other villagers watching from behind the firemen and their hoses as the church building burned down, embers fizzed and leapt worrying close by.

"My brother!" She cried in anguish and the villagers stared at her silently with their blank pale faces.

Less than thirty minutes earlier, Simon had tried to evade Robert's grasping hands, but his own limbs felt fluid and weak. Flailing uselessly, he swung his arms and dislodged one of the candles on the wall which fell onto one of the tiny tacky trees which burned immediately, a pinkish, red mini fireball, almost hypnotic to watch. Burning, it twisted and leant onto its neighbour and caused a domino effect of cheap smouldering and melting plastic, the fumes were stinky and toxic, and both Robert and Simon rushed towards the exit immediately.

Poppy found Simon outside, not long after, seated on a kerb behind the ambulance, a grey blanket draped over his shoulders. His hair was dishevelled and filthy with soot but he seemed fine. Poppy burst into tears when she saw him, crouched down and hugged him. She had not hugged him since they were small children, and she was surprised at the sturdiness of his body and also by the fact that he was trembling.

"Are you alright?" Cried Poppy.

"I am fine, I think…but an ambulance is coming and they said I have to stay here so that they can check me over." Simon sounded both raspy and hollow.

"What about the other kids?"

"Oh, they had already left."

"So, who else was in there with you?"

"Robert, the pastor." There was an edge to Simon's voice, and Poppy glanced at him sharply. "Did he get out?" He asked. Poppy had the weird impression that he was asking merely because he should, not because he cared. The question was a formality.

Bernice, calling home from the hospital in Cavershall, was surprised that Poppy didn't pick up the phone. Maybe, she had her music on loud and didn't hear it ring, she reasoned to herself, although that didn't make much sense under the circumstances.

The doctor had informed Bernice that Peter had suffered a mild heart attack, but that he was stable now. They would be keeping him in for at least a week for observation. Bernice sighed deeply. A small selfish part of her silently bemoaned the fact that they would be stuck in that blasted village for another week at the very least.

A nurse smiled sweetly at her and led her to Peter's room.

83

Peter was in a room on his own and he was awake, albeit unnaturally pale, his skin slick with a clammy sweat. He was wearing a standard issue hospital gown, various tubes and wires protruding from his arms and his chest, and a heart monitor next to his bed recorded his heart beat.

"You can't stay long, he needs to rest." The nurse told Bernice sternly and Bernice nodded dumbly, immediately transfixed by the monotonous beeping sound. Peter suddenly, to her eyes, looked extremely elderly there under the harsh hospital lighting and for one second Bernice couldn't believe that she herself was married to such an old man.

She reached out to hold his hand and his skin felt dry and papery.

"How do you feel?"

"Odd, just very odd and exhausted." He spoke quietly.

"No pain?"

"Oh, there was definitely pain down my arm and in my chest, but not anymore now."

He was obviously too tired to chat, so Bernice sat there holding his hand lightly and within minutes, Peter's eyes closed and his breathing deepened. She too, let herself relax for just a few minutes before being ushered out by the nurse. She retrieved Peter's car keys from his trousers which were neatly folded in the cabinet beside him, and another taxi drove Bernice to the carpark of the factory to collect the car. It seemed to be sitting there alone in that vast freezing space like a forgotten child.

Back in Constance, Simon had been examined by paramedics and pronounced fit, but given strict instructions to go immediately to hospital if his breathing should take a turn for the worse. He was examined inside an ambulance, one of several that had pulled up to the burnt-out husk of the church hall.

The fire was out, but the toxic smell of burning plastic lingered and would do for days if not weeks. The villagers huddled in groups, almost all clad in pyjamas with their winter coats slung over the top and their arms drawn tightly across their chests. It seemed to Poppy that they regarded her with some hostility, that was how she felt. The way they looked at her lacked any kind of expression. They would all turn towards her, a wall of emptiness, and then turn back towards each other to mutter and mumble.

Knowing, as she did, that another man had been in the hall with Simon, this 'Robert,' Poppy watched to see if he was brought out of the wreckage, but he wasn't, or if he was, she must have missed it, or perhaps he had left slightly earlier and just gone home, although that seemed unlikely. In any case, she had never met him and did not know what he looked like.

As soon as the paramedics gave Simon the all-clear, Poppy walked him home to the cottage. He was still trembling and she held him under his arm carefully, the villagers staring after them, the night smelling of sulphur.

Back in the cottage, Poppy made Simon drink a huge glass of water and go straight to bed. She didn't know if that was the correct thing to do but it seemed logical somehow. Then, she went and sat in the living room in the dark and waited for her mother to either phone or come back.

84

It would not be until the following day, in the early afternoon, that Poppy and Bernice learnt of the fate of Pastor Robert. The pair were on their way out, about to get into the car in order to visit Peter in hospital. Simon was at home, slouched on the sofa and watching TV. His throat still felt a bit raspy, but beyond that, he was almost back to normal, physically anyway.

Simon's memory replayed the events of the previous evening on repeat however, exactly like some gruesome film. The brilliant flash of the falling candle as it hit the plastic tree, the sweaty grasp of Robert's claw-like hand on his own arm. The shocking heat of the fire, the way it seemed to surge over them both, as if willed by the devil itself.

Simon had not told his mother or sister about any of it. They knew the outlines of the story only; the youth club, a falling candle, a fire. All three of them had been tempted to investigate that morning, to study the ruins, but they had resisted. Simon knew that the presence of the Jensons at the burnt-out church would be perceived as a kind of admission of guilt.

As Poppy and Bernice both opened their car doors then, a neighbour, who had never cared to speak to the family, not even a simple greeting, came up and informed them coldly and with a sickly relish that Pastor Robert's body had been retrieved from the wreckage of the burnt out church, and that cause of death was yet to be determined, but as Simon had been the last person to see Robert alive, it was probable that the police would want to chat to him.

The way the neighbour informed them, her grey gaze directed specifically towards Bernice, in the cold, clipped tone that was ubiquitous in that village, it was apparent that she, probably the whole village too, believed that Simon was directly responsible for Robert's death.

Bernice struggling to keep her expression neutral, didn't deign to reply to the neighbour. She did not want to give the woman the satisfaction of her reaction. She got in the car without a word and slammed the door. Poppy did the same. For some time, they drove in silence. Rain from the previous day had muddied the frozen landscape, but a ray of sun was beaming down and hitting the windscreen of the car so sharply that

Bernice had to squint to drive and edged even more cautiously than usual through the tiny country lanes.

"What do you think really happened in the church last night?" Asked Poppy carefully.

"I think," Bernice chose her words carefully too, "I think that we will probably never know the full story, but as soon as we are far away from this awful place, the better it will be for all of us."

Bernice was more traumatized than she realised about what she thought of as Simon's near miss. She couldn't think about it too deeply or the disturbing imagery would threaten to overwhelm her. When she had finally returned from the hospital the night before, the fire engines had left and she did not drive back past the church, but the night air was thick with a strange chemical smell. Preoccupied as she was, she didn't give it too much thought until, back in the cottage, Poppy, still agitated, explained what had happened.

Immediately then, Bernice had rushed to see Simon. He seemed fine and was breathing deeply in his sleep. He smelt of smoke and of the toxic air outside. To Bernice, he was still her little boy and she sat by his bed all night, watching him breathe, making sure he was really alright.

85

Peter was looking much better. There was some colour in his cheeks and he smiled widely to see Poppy especially. He had always had a soft spot for his daughter.

Bernice was greatly relieved. She had understood from the nurse's careful language, that although Peter seemed to be out of the woods, things could still go either way. That being the case, Bernice and Poppy had decided not to tell Peter about the fire and especially not about Simon's escape from it. They didn't want to cause Peter any further stress.

The nurse insisted that they not stay too long so as not to 'over-excite' Peter, and this suited Bernice perfectly, as her heart's desire was to return to Simon to make sure that he was still and definitely alright. Especially if there was any kind of risk of the police coming round to interrogate him. It was New Year's Day though, Bernice hoped that rural policemen might want to make use of the Bank Holiday before getting to work.

It was hard to stick to bland chit chat with Peter knowing that there had been a death in Constance in which Simon was likely to be implicated. Bernice literally felt as if she had to swallow down the words that rose in her throat and threatened to give the game away. As it was, she had barely slept and her own throat felt dry and gritty too, as did her eyes, probably as a result of the thick fumes still lingering in the air around their cottage. Once again, she was looking at Peter, but distracted by worries about Simon, about his health, about the other villagers circling the cottage like vultures looking for someone to blame for Robert's death.

Robert had been their pastor, their leader. Many of his flock had placed him on an unwarranted pedestal. They had been paying him all their lives to secure their spot in heaven, after all. Who could predict now how they would react? Officially, as far as the Jensons were aware, his was still considered an accidental death. However, that did not mean that the villagers, who had always regarded the Jensons as the enemy, the interlopers at the very least, would not have their own theories. Simon had been given strict instructions not to open the front door to anyone anyway.

As Poppy chatted lightly to Peter about the most painfully superficial topics possible, Bernice was wondering if it would be possible to get Peter transferred directly from this hospital to one near their home in London. As the thought came to her, she felt her spirits tentatively rise. If it was indeed possible and Peter was taken care of, then the rest of them could just pack up the cottage and get the hell out of there in the space of hours.

On the way out of the ward, without sharing her plan with Poppy, Bernice asked the nurse who she would need to speak to in order to arrange hospital transport. She sensed Poppy next to her raise her eyebrows. The nurse provided the name of the man who was in charge of things like that, but added that he was on annual leave and would not be around until the third of January.

"In any case," added the nurse in a disapproving tone, "We would not recommend moving Peter until the end of the week at the very least."

Bernice nodded tersely. She fervently hoped that they could lie low for at least a few more days in the cottage without attracting more drama.

86

It was early the following morning when a police car pulled up outside the cottage. There was no siren, but the chirp of the police radio was loud on the silent road as the doors opened and two hefty policemen got out.

Poppy, at the living room window heard it and was the first to see them approach. She rushed to tell her mother. Behind the police car, in the frozen pale light of a January morning, a few villagers were gathering in their black coats, like hyenas. The scent of fire still perfumed the air. It had not yet rained.

Bernice was in her new thick flannel dressing gown that Peter had given her as a Christmas present. Christmas felt so long ago then, and as if it had happened to someone else.

"Shit! But Simon's still asleep!" Bernice started shaking with panic immediately and Poppy laid a hand on her arm, shocked as she was that her own mother couldn't seem to cope with this situation.

"Go! Get dressed, wake Simon, I'll get the door!"

By then there was a loud knocking, too intrusive and insistent to seem casual. When Poppy opened the door, however, still in pyjamas herself and looking young without make-up, the policemen were kindly and polite though, merely stating that they wished to take Simon's statement about what had occurred in the church on the night of the fire.

They were both large, hefty men, one slightly younger, the other wrinkled and bald. The older one explained that they had come from the nearest police station which was based in Tensit.

Poppy seated them in the uncomfortable living room where they seemed to absorb all the space and she made a big deal of offering them tea. Bernice came down, neatly dressed and twitchy with nerves and Simon slouched in behind her still in his pyjamas.

There was something about the expression on her brother's face, at that moment and in the moments that followed, that unnerved Poppy. It was as if he had retreated behind a mask. He answered each question politely, but he was acting. The persona on display was not his. Uncannily the blankness on his face resembled, in some ways, that on the faces of the villagers, a brutish stillness. Poppy was afraid to catch her mother's eye, of course they were both implicated in this act, because now she was sure that it was, indeed, an act.

Simon stuck to the same script. He repeated the same thing that he had told his mother and his sister countless times which was simple and hard to poke holes in. A candle had fallen and set fire to one of the plastic trees. Simon himself was so intent on escaping that he didn't even look around to see where Robert was. He was just leaving in any case, had just said goodbye to the pastor and Happy New Year. Simon never saw Robert as he dashed out of the burning building, so intent he was on saving himself. That was his story and he reiterated it in many ways and, to Poppy's ears, sounded very convincing.

Simon's voice sounded a bit raspy, but beyond that you would never be able to tell what he had been through. He looked shiny and clean and honest.

Unless you already knew him, thought Poppy, and then the truth was altogether far more alarming.

Bernice asked the policemen whether an autopsy would be carried out on Robert and she was informed that it would, but that the body was in terrible condition so they probably wouldn't be able to find anything concrete or useful.

Poppy found that she had crossed her fingers.

The policemen made Simon sign his statement, which he did with a steady hand. On the way out of the door, they wished the Jensons, automatically, a Happy New Year.

87

Later that day, in the early afternoon, just before Poppy and Bernice set off to see Peter, Emily came to the door and Poppy, after careful surveillance from the window, let her in. Poppy had only glimpsed her before from a distant, but it was clear from Emily's tentative knocking on the door that she was not one of the vindictive villagers.

Simon came bounding down the stairs. He was clearly expecting her. Emily, pallid and slim, her hair loose about her shoulders and framing her tiny face, resembled to Poppy's eyes, some wan Victorian maiden. She mumbled hello to Poppy and smiled shyly. Simon led the way to his room up the stairs and Poppy heard Emily tell him that she couldn't stay long, that she was supposed to be elsewhere. Clearly, Emily had to lie to her parents about seeing Simon.

Poppy and Bernice drove off to Cavershall leaving the young couple in the house. They both chuckled about that, and made jokes about young love in a rare, albeit fleeting, moment of levity. Minutes later, they both grew sombre again. A light freezing drizzle permeated the air. Bernice was relieved that finally the toxic smoke in the village would be cleansed. She drove carefully, mindful that the unsophisticated roads might be slippery. Poppy was wondering whether Simon was also lying to Emily, and if he was, to what extent.

It wasn't until the morning of the following day, the 3rd of January, that the police showed up again at the cottage. It was the same two policemen as before, and as before a motley little crew of villagers could be seen in a huddle further down the road. This time, there was something in the stillness of their stance and the sharpness of their glances that reminded Poppy of crows.

Simon was dressed this time and as distantly affable as before. The older policeman, sitting in the living room again, informed them that the state of Robert's body was such that it would be impossible to conduct a forensic examination in the facilities they had locally. Had they had any evidence of foul play, they would have transported his body to London where the labs were much more sophisticated, but the CPS had ruled that such a transfer was unwarranted, that there was no such evidence. In conclusion, the death of Robert had been ruled as accidental, and there would be no further investigation.

Poppy had been holding her breath throughout that entire speech and rigidly controlling the neutral expression on her own face. Careful not to look directly at either her mother of her brother, she could nevertheless see Simon's face out of the corner of her eye, because of where he was perched in the living room.

At the time, such a profound relief flooded through Poppy, that all she could think about was that her brother was in the clear, they were all now free to leave. It was only later that night, in her mind's eye, that she was revisited by the smooth blankness of Simon's expression in that moment and disconcerted by it. More than that, Poppy was disturbed by her brother's new effortless skill at acting and further disturbed by the idea of what he may have done.

That afternoon, all three of the Jensons visited Peter. Simon was no longer coughing and Peter had requested repeatedly to see him. Bernice had told Peter that Simon couldn't visit him at the hospital because he had a cold, but Peter had seemed unconvinced by the lie, and seemed much buoyed by the sight of Simon in his hospital room.

They had agreed, on the drive to Cavershall, that they would tell Peter about the fire at the church, he was, in any case, likely to find out. Bernice recounted the story, therefore to Peter as he sat up in bed looking much recovered. The story Bernice told, however, bore little resemblance to the truth. In the story, Simon had no involvement whatsoever. Due to his 'cold,' he had not attended the youth club party that night, he had stayed at home, and therefore, everything the Jensons knew about the fire and about Robert's death, they knew as indifferent observers.

For the second time that day, Poppy struggled to maintain an expression of neutrality on her face.

"Oh my gosh, what a drama!" Peter looked shocked and turned immediately to Simon who was perched on the end of his hospital bed.

"Did your friends get out alright? Was anyone injured?"

"They had all left already, that is what I was told."

"Phew, what a relief!"

88

The man who organised hospital transfers was back from his holiday, and Bernice, after some tedious back and forth, had organised that Peter would be transferred on the 6th of January to the hospital in London closest to their house. Poppy therefore arranged that she would travel back to Nottingham that day too and move into halls. Finally, after all the drama of the previous days, she allowed herself to feel excited by the prospect of that.

Bernice and Simon decided to leave early on that morning as well, to drive back to London, which meant that, on the 5th of January, the Jensons spent all day packing and did not go to see Peter. They bid him farewell on the day before and arranged to see him in London, every bit as excited as if they were organising a fun outing instead of arranging to meet in the ward of another hospital in another city. Poppy promised to return to London to see Peter soon, it was much closer to Nottingham than Constance was.

Both Poppy and Bernice had repeatedly told Simon that he could not just vanish from Constance without a word to Emily, it was heartless and cruel.

"Does she have any idea that you intend to leave and return to London? Even that dad has left the factory?" Poppy had asked him, to which Simon had just shrugged. Poppy felt a frustrated heat rise to her face. Her brother had previously always been annoying in the normal way of brothers, this show of cold-hearted indifference, however, was entirely new and unpleasant.

"Perhaps he picked that attitude up from the other kids here." Remarked Bernice grimly when Poppy shared her concerns. "He used to complain that they were all unfeeling and heartless at school every day, when he was there. Perhaps, he caught it off them like a bug."

It was more than that, thought Poppy. Her brother was starting to give her the creeps.

Grudgingly, he finally agreed to say a proper goodbye to Emily, and with that in mind, he organised for her to come round to the cottage on that last day, when they were packing.

As soon as she walked in, to see the boxes everywhere, stacked up in the hall, Emily looked completely confused and shocked.

"Where are you going?" She asked in a small voice, and her tone tugged at Poppy's heart strings. It was clear that the poor child had no idea, and Simon had just been planning to leave her without saying a word. Bernice and Poppy stayed downstairs as the couple went upstairs for some privacy but Poppy could still hear Emily crying. She looked at her mother but Bernice was pretending not to hear. Her mouth was set in a thin hard line.

All the way back to university, on that endless journey through a bleak, frozen January landscape, Poppy thought about her brother. She couldn't stop thinking about Simon, although the memory of the indifference on his face was making her feel ill.

He had never been like that before.

Simon and Bernice, on their own long journey back to London in the car, chatted about all they had missed there; simple things about their house or their neighbourhood.

After a while, a pensive silence fell over them like a cloud. Bernice started worrying about money, because that was a real and pressing concern. After the euphoria of the move home had died down, it would be sure to hit them like a brick.

Simon stared out of the window at the cars zooming past on the motorway, at the monotonous muddy green fields. He thought about his last moments in the burning church before he had escaped, they replayed often in his mind. He thought about how floppy his arms and legs had felt and yet how he had summoned the last vestiges of his strength and swung his fist at Robert's head, and how Robert had fallen flat down on his back as the flames edged closer, just like a felled tree. He had been unconscious certainly. Simon had bent over his ugly face and checked before running out.

THE END

Printed in Dunstable, United Kingdom